The Youn

# The Young at Heart

Award Winning Stories for Readers of All Ages

by

Chastine E. Shumway

Illustrations by Jan Stratton

iUniverse, Inc.
New York Bloomington

iUniverse books may be ordered through booksellers or by contacting:

iUniverse
1663 Liberty Drive
Bloomington, IN 47403
www.iuniverse.com
1-800-Authors (1-800-288-4677)

ISBN: 978-1-4401-8854-1 (sc)
ISBN: 978-1-4401-8855-8 (ebook)

Printed in the United States of America

iUniverse rev. date: 4/5/2010

# Dedication

This book is gratefully dedicated to GOD who has given me heaven on earth. HE has blessed me with a wonderful family, Christian friends, and loyal readers.

To my Shumway children: Sandy, Dick, Art, Susie, Florence and Betty.

To my Daughter-in laws Beverly Shumway and Robin Shumway.

To my grandchildren: Candace, Erik, Jacob, Jennifer, Rick, Rachael, Kris, Akisha, Breanna, Russell, Frederick, Maria, Chastine (my namesake), Chastine, Victoria Rose and Eddie. To my great-grandsons, Devon, Reese, Will, Grant and Simmons.

Front Cover

Top: Chastine Franklin
Left: Maria Brummett
Right: Victoria Rose Franklin

The girls are holding their famous
American Girl ˚ Dolls

Back Cover
Top Picture

( top left – right)
Betty Franklin, Arthur Shumway
(Bottom left-right)
Mayor Shelly Davis, Chastine Shumway

Bottom Picture
Mayor Davis presenting a proclamation, honoring Chastine and her
collection of writing from over the years, declaring that a day be set aside to
be celebrated annually on April 20th as "The Unforgettable Day" in honor
of Ms. Chastine E. Shumway

(left – right)
Mayor Shelly Davis, Chastine Shumway

# Introduction

## YOUNG AT HEART

Do you have magic in your heart? Then this book was written for you. Do you know what young at heart means? It means no matter how old or young you are, the exuberance of life has never left you. Writing these stories and newspaper articles has been a source of enjoyment and pleasure for me through my life.

Most of the stories in this book have won awards and have been published in magazines. These stories are divided into sections, which include fairy tales, true history stories, fiction and nonfiction stories for the Young at Heart of all ages.

Literature is entertaining. It is idealistic, and it helps you to dream, sometimes making your dreams come true. So join me as we journey together in the land of make believe, true adventures, and the history of our great land, America!

# Contents

Who Sez?...1

Adventures of King McElf...2

Nola Mae, The Eye Book, And Ugly ...10

The Three Little Monkeys...16

The Lonesome Old Man...19

Delta Black Boy's Adventure...22

Delta Black Boy And Big Ole Kat...26

Zophana, The Colorful Man...31

Rolling With The Punches...32

Ozark Recollections...34

An Unbelievable Horse...39

The Two Soldiers Of Fortune, The Horse And Soldier...42

A Military Love Story...48

The Members of the Greely Expedition in 1881...67

# Who Sez?

Who sez there aren't fairies?

Not I. I wouldn't dare! Not that I have ever seen a shimmering little fairy belle peeking out at me from a fluorescent rainbow. But they're out there I tell you. You can bet your boots on that!

Who sez angels only live in heaven, and we will never see them until we get there.

Not I. I wouldn't dare! Mama tells me that she sees angels all the time. I asked her where they were, and she smiled and said, "Well you are one of my little angels."

And you know what? Looking at Mama's serene face, I knew right then and there that I lived with an angel.

Who sez the wee people aren't out there? Like a sassy little elf with his hands on his hips. Not I. I wouldn't dare! When I feel like visiting my magic place, I quietly step lightly and go to my rambling rose and vine covered arbor in our back yard. I have to stoop down so I don't catch my hair in the thorns. And also I watch where my feet land. I just know the wee people were sipping dewdrop tea from the sunshiny buttercups the night before. And you can see where they have spilled some drops on the large toadstool they used for a table. They heard me coming, and they're hiding in the blades of grass, but I think they might have hopped a ride with the red bird that just flew by. As the wind blew through the leaves, I think I heard their tinkling laughter.

Yes there's magic all around us. Just close your eyes and listen very carefully.

Did you feel something brush across your face? That was a fairy kissing you. Did you hear a jingling sound? Was that just the wind? You might think it was, but not I!

# Adventures of King McElf

*This story won at Ole Miss College with a rated book publisher, who said it was very clever and to market it.*

Squiddly Dee and Squiddly Squee,

Come out and play with me.

Squiddly Dee, Squiddly Squee

We'll have lots of fun; you'll see!"

Victoria Rose was asleep when she heard a soft, tinkling voice singing. Was she dreaming? She opened her green eyes just a little. The big full moon was shining through her bedroom window, which was open. A warm gentle breeze whispered softly as the organdy curtains billowed like an airy cloud over her bed. She snuggled deeper in her plump feather bed and closed her eyes again.

Something began tickling her little pug nose. Was it a pesky fly? She swatted it. She felt something silky. She could not let it go. It was stuck to her hand. Her eyes popped open. Her hand held a cobweb. She took her other hand and grabbed the web to pull it off. Now both hands were imprisoned. Then the cobweb grew wider and wider. It yanked her out of bed swinging her through the open window and over the brick garden wall. She landed feet first, right smack dab in the middle of her mother's rose garden.

"Doggies," an irritated voice groaned, "Get your big foot off my coattail. Can't anyone enjoy a cup of tea without a body ruining it?"

Victoria Rose looked down. There was a strange little man, dressed in a coat of green leaves. He was sitting on a toadstool. He was no bigger than the birds in the sky. She started laughing. "You must be an elf."

The little man screwed up his face and mocked her. "You must be an elf. Ha, Ha, very funny." Twisting his face into a scowl, he got up, and putting

his hands on his hips said, "What's so funny about being an elf?" Taking his curled up pointed elfin shoe, he kicked her big toe.

"Oh," she laughed again. "That tickled, but you should mind your manners and never kick a lady." Stooping over, she grabbed him and held him up looking at him eye to eye. "If anyone should be angry, it should be me. Was it you who was singing and woke me up from a beautiful dream, and using your elfin magic made the cobweb grow into a rope to kidnap me?"

The tears began to fall. As they fell, the little elf quickly snatched them up, putting them into a small pouch around his waist.

Victoria gave him a squeeze and threw him towards the ground. With a pout on her face, she said, "Go ahead and drink your tea. I'm leaving." She tossed her golden curls, and with her head held high she turned to leave. The little elf had a small pair of wings and instead of landing on the ground, he flew up and perched on her shoulder.

In a soothing voice, he crooned, "Now, now, everything is all right. My name is King McElf. I've watched you play in the garden with your friends. You are so much fun, I wanted to invite you to Elfinville to keep me company."

"You're very kind, Mr. King McElf, but I can't leave my mama and papa, and besides I am like a giant compared to you. If we play together I might accidentally squash you."

3

King McElf scratched his head, as if he were in deep thought. "There, there." he said as he pulled a feather from his cocky hat and tapped her cheek with it. "Just come to Elfinville with me until morning. Then you can go home. No one will miss you."

Feeling a little lightheaded, she said, "Is that a promise, Mr. King McElf?"

"A promise?" A mischievous grin crept over his face. "Yes, whatever a promise is." Flying down to the ground where clumps of yellow buttercups were, he picked one. "Here's a cup of teardrop tea. Drink, little princess, it will make you feel better." He held it up to her ruby red lips.

She sipped a little. The tea smelled and tasted like fresh rain. It sent her senses reeling. Feeling faint she put her hand on her forehead. "Oh dear!" she sighed. She could not bear to look at what was happening to her. Her mama had told her never to accept anything from strangers, and now King McElf had tricked her. When the whirling motion stopped, she opened her eyes. She was standing on the rim of the birdbath looking directly into Mr. McElf's eyes. The water in the bowl looked like a mirror, and she saw her reflection. What she saw surprised her. She was the same size as King McElf, and she was no longer in her pajamas. She was adorned in a gown of emerald green silk with hundreds of sparkling dewdrops woven in and out of spidery lace. The beautiful gown twinkled like the stars in the sky. On her feet were crystal clear glass slippers. But she didn't have any wings. "How did I get here King McElf? I don't have any wings to fly."

Scratching his head, he said, "Someday you will have your wings. But if you hold a fairy's or elves hand, you will be able to fly."

King McElf was dressed differently too. He was decked out in a small tuxedo. He stood looking at her. Admiration filled his eyes. "Time's awasting my beautiful princess." He grabbed her hand, and they flew over to a tall hollyhock.

Victoria Rose exclaimed, "Oh what fun it is to fly!"

They landed at the roots of the lanky red flower. Victoria Rose had never seen this flower in the garden before. "How do Ms. Holly." King McElf tipped his top hat.

Ms. Holly in her red dress bent over in a sweeping bow, whispering, "Enter, my King."

King McElf and Victoria Rose entered through the center of the flower and slid down a dark tunnel weaving in and out of the roots. They were moving so fast, just like a roller coaster. Victoria Rose was frightened. She covered her eyes.

"Open your eyes, my little Princess," King McElf said. We have arrived."

They were in a land of bright sunshine. Colorful feathered birds were singing in the swaying trees. Butterflies flitted from flower to flower kissing them. It was a dazzling and delightful sight. A rainbow arched across the sky surrounded by shooting stars. At the beginning of the rainbow, stood a splendid carriage with teensy white horses decorated with plumes and jingling bells, prancing eagerly. King McElf led Victoria Rose to the carriage and extended his hand to her. She stepped daintily into the carriage. The butterflies formed a cluster flying ahead of the carriage leading them up and over the rainbow path.

Victoria Rose rubbed her eyes. She could not believe what was happening to the butterflies. They had turned into hundreds of little people with transparent wings. "Why the butterflies have turned into fairies and elves!" she exclaimed.

In small singing voices, they chanted, "Long live the King and his Queen to be!" Then they began dancing and sliding over the rainbow.

King McElf smiled an elfish grin and arched his little eyebrows. "Remember the butterfly who lit on your cheek while you were playing with your friends yesterday?

She nodded and said, "Oh yes, I do remember."

He said, "That was me."

"Where are we going Mr. King McElf?" Victoria asked.

"Soon you will see Victoria Rose. We will be at our destination when we come to the end of the rainbow."

Victoria Rose could not wait! All of a sudden bright colored glowing lights appeared, flashing off and on, shooting sprays of stars from the rainbow into the heavens. It was an awesome display.

King McElf said, "Now we are at the end of the rainbow. We have arrived." At the base of the rainbow stood a gleaming pot of shining gold. It was filled with jewels. King McElf climbed down from the carriage and picked out a pearl ring for Victoria. He placed it on her finger. In a very low whisper he said, "To my Queen of Elfinville. We will reign together forever!"

Victoria was not paying attention, and she didn't hear a word of what he said. "Oh look." She pointed to a majestic castle standing on a hill. The little horses were trotting at a fast pace towards it. "Why are so many little people dressed in dress up clothes? Are they celebrating something special?"

King McElf said, "They're celebrating your arrival to the Elfinville's Ball."

Trumpets blasted as they crossed the moat. The carriage stopped at the palace entrance. Four little elves approached them with canopied chairs. Victoria Rose and King McElf climbed onto them, and the elves lifted the chairs up into the air. As they were being carried into the palace, an elf danced in front of them playing a flute with a merry tune. Victoria Rose noticed that all kinds of musical instruments danced through the air playing a familiar tune without musicians. Victoria Rose was delighted, because her music box in her room played the same tune, The Toy Soldiers.

Soon they were in an elaborate ballroom with hanging sparkling crystal chandeliers. Fairies and elves were dancing and eating, but when King and Victoria Rose arrived, everything grew quiet. The canopied chairs were placed on the mirrored floor. King McElf took Victoria Rose's little hand and led her towards two thrones. One throne had King McElf's name on it, and much to Victoria's surprise the other throne had her name as Queen Victoria Rose on it.

Standing up proudly, King McElf announced, "This is Victoria Rose. She is going to be my Queen." Pulling her from her throne, he placed a sparkling bejeweled crown on her head, saying, "We will soon rule Elfinville together." The little people applauded.

Victoria Rose gently took the crown from her head and handed it back to the King and in a serious voice said, "King McElf, you promised that I would be home by morning. I can not be your Queen."

The fairies and elves gasped. "The King promised her she could go home? A King cannot go back on his word."

King McElf was furious. His little head broke out in beads of sweat. His face became beet red with anger. He acted unkingly. He jumped up and down. In a trembling voice, he said, "How dare you refuse me!"

Just then loud bells began to toll. This was a sign of danger. Screams pierced the air. The sound of the bells abruptly came to a halt. The Elves and Fairies panicked. "The goblins are here! The goblins are here! Save us, oh King."

Trying to see what was happening, Victoria Rose whispered, "What's happening King McElf?"

"Never fear Victoria Rose. My army and I shall protect you and my subjects. Hide behind the drapes until I call for you."

King McElf jerked his sword from its sheath and held it up high. Sparks and bright blinding flashes leaped from his sword. This did not faze the goblins, as their eyes were glass. Then hundreds of cobwebs appeared and fell from the palace ceiling, growing into strong ropes.

At first the goblins were in a stupor and didn't know what to do, but their goblin leader screeched and laughed an eerie laugh until his face turned purple. He grabbed a cobweb rope and swung up to where King McElf stood, knocking the little king down. He quickly tied the king up.

The King's magic sword slid across the floor right where Victoria was hiding. She jumped out from her hiding place and grabbed the sword. Facing the ugly goblin leader she yelled in a loud voice, "STOP!" The Goblins came to a halt. The cobweb ropes returned to their original silky selves leaving the Goblins who had climbed and swung on them sprawled all over the floor.

The leader, Goblin Bad Blood, stood with his hands on his hips and a dark grin spread across his face. His hair was a blazing red. On the end of his tail was a third hand.

Victoria commanded in a loud voice, "Goblins, be gone!" Victoria waved the sword. Nothing happened.

King McElf, lying on the floor with his little wings tied down, moaned. "Victoria Rose, the sword only works for me. Woe is me!"

When Goblin Bad Blood heard this, he swung his tail with the hand on it jerking the sword from Victoria's hand. Wiggling his eyebrows up and down, he asked, "Where did you find this spunky wench, McElf?" He circled Victoria. "I'll make a deal with you, McElf. I'll trade your life and your subject's lives for this pretty maiden."

King McElf rolled over and over frantically trying to get loose and saying bravely, "No, Goblin Bad Blood. She's the future queen of Elfinville. Kill me if you wish, but when you do, all of your goblin band will be struck stone dead. Leave us in peace."

Victoria was trembling. She cried, "No, King McElf. I will go with him, if it will save you and your kingdom."

Goblin Bad Blood grabbed Victoria and slung her over his shoulder like a sack of flour. "I am taking her with me. You and your subjects have your lives." Then he strutted towards the palace door.

Victoria yelled. She pounded him on his back with both her fists. "Put me down!" Goblin Bad Blood just laughed his hideous laugh.

Victoria Rose's teeth began to chatter out of sheer fear. She began to cry. And Victoria was not crying softly. She was howling. Her cries echoed loudly, so loud, that the castle walls shook. Her tears were falling like sheets of rain.

Goblin Bad Blood could not stand the noisy sobs, and he put her down at the door. He said, "Stop, I can't stand this bellowing."

Victoria couldn't control herself. The harder she tried to quit crying, the worse her wailing became. The tears were covering the floor. The more she thought about not seeing her mama or papa again, the harder she cried. Something strange was happening to her now. Every time her tears touched her feet, she was lifted above what was becoming a lake of tears.

Now the Goblins could not fly, because only good things fly and they couldn't swim like fish do, so the tears got so deep that the goblins were covered completely. Goblin Bad Blood forgot about Victoria. He was splashing and thrashing about in the sea of tears, trying to save himself, but they soon covered him. A strong wind began to blow. It swirled into a black funnel like a twister and swooped all the tears together. The swirling twister sucked the evil goblins up, whirling them through the palace door away from Elfinville.

Meanwhile King McElf had gotten loose and was flying around looking frantically for Victoria Rose. He and his subjects could not find her. They finally gave up believing that Victoria had drowned in the sea of tears. The King and all the wee folk were mourning for her, sitting with their heads bowed low in sorrow. Then there was a sound of fluttering wings. Looking up, King McElf cried, "It's Victoria Rose! You have your wings for saving our lives." All the wee people whose wings were torn off by Bad Blood's band of Goblins had their wings back too and began singing and thanking her.

"She is back, she is back.
Our precious Queen to be,
She will keep us safe from harm, and we will live in harmony."

Victoria Rose looked sad. "No my little friends, I must go home. I shall miss everyone, but I must go home."

King McElf patted her hand saying, "You would make a fine queen. You saved Elfinville and its people. I'm sorry I frightened you with my angry words. I did give you my word that you would be home in the morning.

The Elves and the Fairies groaned.

"I want to grant you your wish. A King cannot go back on his word, but I do not have my magic sword to do so."

Then the Fairies and Elves smiled and were happy. They clapped their little hands. They whispered, "She cannot go home. Our queen must stay. The King does not have his magic sword."

King McElf's eyes lit up. By losing his sword he was gaining Victoria Rose as his queen. He took Victoria's hand in his and looking into her eyes said, "I want to keep my word, but without the sword, it's impossible, but my subjects and I will make you very happy."

The Fairies and Elves began singing and dancing.
"She is back, she is back.
Our Precious Queen to be
Now we will live in harmony

Victoria smiled. "Thank you King McElf and my little friends for your kind thoughts, but don't despair. I have a surprise for you. As Goblin Bad Blood was being covered with my tears, he lost your sword. I grabbed it as it floated by." She reached into her pocket and pulled the little flashing sword out, and handed it to the king.

The Fairies and Elves moaned. One little fairy flew up to Victoria's shoulder and said, "Will you promise to visit us again?"

Victoria Rose nodded her head in a yes. Then she turned toward King McElf and kissed him on his cheek.

His face grew red. He said, "Someday you shall be my Queen." King McElf continued, "A day in Elfinville is like a year." He took her hand with the ring sparkling on her finger and said, "Rub the ring Victoria." Then he touched her with his sword. "You'll get home just as I promised."

"Victoria Rose, what are you doing in the garden? We have looked and looked for you." It was her mama with papa looking down at her.

Papa laughed saying; "Our little girl must have walked in her sleep."

Something was scratching Victoria's neck. She raised her hand to see what it was. It was a bright shiny needle in her pajama collar. It looked like a miniature sword. Then a butterfly brushed her cheek as it floated away. Victoria smiled. She knew it wasn't a dream. She knew she would always be in touch with Elfinville.

# Nola Mae,
# The Eye Book, And Ugly

### By
### Chastine Ellen Shumway

Nola Mae was not your average old woman mind you. For one thing she did not know she was old. After getting dressed every morning in a red dress, she wore a big red bow to match in her white hair. She looked in the mirror every morning after she cleaned up and would call to her hill parrot Ugly, "Who is that old woman looking at me?" Ugly's cage door was always open, so he could fly or hop or walk anyplace he wanted to go. He flew to Nola Mae's shoulder and looked in the mirror. Ugly squawked loudly and said, "Don't know Nola Mae, Don't know!"

Nola Mae said, "That's what I know."

Then he said, "Who is that old funny looking bird with the big beak and the gray beard looking at me Nola Mae?"

Nola Mae said, "Don't know Ugly. Don't know!"

Then Ugly flew back to his cage and laughed like a parrot laughs and turned somersaults.

Nola Mae and Ugly now lived in a stone house on the side of a big mountain. They didn't always live in this stone house. Tall pine trees stood like soldiers guarding their little stone house. Strong winds had come all through the mountains, but the forces of nature never blew their stone house down. All kinds of birds nested in the trees. Lordly deer visited their timbered woods everyday. There was a spring that never stopped flowing with crystal clear water for them to drink. All kinds of fish swam and leaped in the air in a pond that the spring had created. This was a happy place, but Nola Mae was sad. She never smiled. And there was a reason.

Ugly and Nola Mae planted a garden in the springtime when the moon was round and bright in the middle of the night when everyone was asleep.

Nola Mae rolled her wheelplow through the dirt making narrow crevices. Ugly carried the seeds in his large bill and dropped them in the earth openings. Mr. Beaver with his large flat tail followed behind them sweeping the dirt over the top of the seeds.

When summer came, neighbors came to look at their garden. There was a reason they came. They had gardens too. But their garden never looked as good as Nola Mae's. The deer, rabbits, and squirrels chomped up all their lettuce, radishes, and green beans and the tomatoes. To frighten the animals away from their gardens they hung tin cans from the trees, which rattled in the wind. They made scarecrows with hands flapping in the wind, but that did not help. The animals didn't like this, so the neighbor's gardens looked like a war zone. The neighboring women were upset, because they did not have enough vegetables to can for the winter.

Nola Mae's garden remained green and flourished with vegetables. She had a big heart and always shared what she had with her neighbors. In one corner of Nola Mae's garden was a large section of lettuce. In the middle of this patch was a sign with a picture of a rabbit on it. All the rabbits congregated in this patch because they knew Nola Mae and Ugly made it especially for them. The magical happening about the rabbits eating all of the lettuce and carrots was that overnight the vegetables grew again.

When neighbors came to visit, they always left with all kinds of fruits and vegetables. But still Nola Mae never smiled. And there was a reason. There was a mystery about Nola Mae and Ugly, and there was only one person who knew the secret. That was Miss Jean, the librarian, who had 'The Eye Book'. Now some hill folk are part elves and part humans. Not all of them mind you, but some of them are. And Miss Jean was one of them. Miss Jean knew that if she ever revealed the secret, she would turn into one of the round boulders in the forest, which had no hearts. There was a reason Miss Jean had The Eye Book. She and 'The Eye Book' became friends. At night she would close the blinds of the library, making sure the doors were locked and take 'The Eye Book' out of the safe. Before daylight, she would look around cautiously, wrap it up and slip it back in the safe. No one knew the combination but her. There is a reason Miss Jean had The Eye Book and it told her this story.

"One day an old mountain man called Hunter got lost in the mountains. He was hunting one beautiful winter day when a blizzard began covering the ground with snow. All of a sudden there appeared a huge golden buck with an unbelievable rack a few feet from Hunter. He whispered to himself. "I have to have this buck for a trophy. I will be rich having a golden deer." He raised his gun and fired. He missed. The buck bounded gracefully up the mountain. Hunter knew he should head back to the village because the snow was getting deeper, but he had never seen a buck like this. He had to have him. It would be the talk of the village, and he would have it as a trophy on his wall. The buck proudly stood out in the open. He didn't move. Hunter's eyelashes were almost frozen shut. Blinded, he belly crawled up the mountain. Although he was weak and his vision was blurred, he slowly raised his gun aiming it at this golden buck. He fired. That's all he remembered.

When he heard a melodious voice he thought he had died and was in heaven with an angel. He opened his eyes. There was a young girl with a bowl of hot porridge. With a smile on her lips, she whispered, "Eat, this will be good for you."

The old man sat up and did as she said and was in awe of the young girl's beauty. On her shoulder sat a parrot, who said, "My name is Ugly!"

After he finished eating, the young girl brought over a book called The Eye Book. On the cover of the book was a picture of a huge open eye with its one eyeball moving in all directions. She opened the book. Inside the book was a picture of a girl that looked like her. Her name was under the picture. It was Nola Mae. She was sitting on the floor with Ugly on her shoulder. Beside them in the picture stood a handsome young man. Hunter asked, "Who is this man?"

Nola Mae demurely bowed her head and blushed. Ugly flew in circles losing some of his feathers and squawking. "Why it's you Hunter. It's you! You've finally come back."

Hunter laughed, but it was not his old crackled voice. It was a laugh of someone young. Nola Mae held up a mirror and showed him his face. Hunter looked. He was young again. "No!" he yelled. The cave echoed his voice. "No! No! No! That is I when I was young. I am dreaming! I am dreaming!"

Nola Mae said, "You are still young Hunter, and I still love you."

Hunter was thinking. She is beautiful. I will take her home with me.

The next morning, he told Nola Mae that they were going to play a game. It was called "Blind Man's Bluff."

Nola Mae said, "Oh I love to play games."

Ugly squawked, "No, Nola Mae, Don't believe him. He wants to take you away. He left you once, and if you leave our mountain bad things will happen."

Nola Mae didn't listen. She was in love with Hunter.

Hunter said, "I will put this cloth over your face because you are the blind person in this game." Hunter put a cloth over her face and led her out of the cave. It was a pretty day. The snow was gone, but the golden buck was standing on a cliff watching them.

Looking up at him, Hunter called out, "I will be back to get you later." Hunter picked Nola Mae up and headed down the mountain. The cloth veil slipped, and she saw that they were a long way from her cave home. She began crying and yelling.

"Ugly!" The bird flew out of the cave and dove all over Hunter's head, pecking at his eyes." Then Ugly lit on Nola Mae's head, calling, "Nola Mae I am here. I will take care of you." She stopped crying.

When they got to the village, Hunter took his bride to be straight to the library. Miss Jean was expecting them, as she had heard about the happening in the wind.

Hunter said, "Look at me Miss Jean how young I am, and look at my beautiful young bride to be."

Hunter lifted the veil off of Nola Mae's face. He jumped back. Nola Mae was not the beautiful young girl he had tricked into coming. This was an old toothless hag. He jumped back as she smiled at him. He yelled, "I've been tricked. Look Miss Jean, look at me. I am young and handsome again."

Miss Jean pulled out a mirror from her desk drawer. "Hunter you are dreaming. You still look like you always did."

He looked into the mirror. He was looking at an old man. He said, "Miss Jean look at 'The Eye Book'. It will show you pictures." When he opened the book where the girl's picture had been, there was just a blank page. He scratched his head in disbelief and said, "I can't understand it. Her picture and my picture was in the book at the cave. We were both young."

Miss Jean nodded her head knowingly. She said, "Nola Mae is here, not there anymore, but her home and heart will always be in the mountain cave home. She will never smile again. The Eye Book knows that." With that statement, she closed the book and said, "Nola Mae will never be young or happy again until she returns to her mountain cave home."

The Eye Book had tears dripping from it.

Hunter ran out of the library screaming uncontrollably. No one could understand his blabbering. He had gone mad. After that happening no one ever saw Hunter again.

In back of Nola Mae's and Ugly's new home was an orchard. In the orchard were apple trees, cherry trees and pear trees. No one knew how the orchard got there. In the spring, white clusters of flowers appeared on the branches of the apple tree. Nola Mae and Ugly enjoyed smelling the sweet fragrance of these trees. Then after the wind blew away the flowers, there appeared beautiful red apples. And the strange part of this story is when Nola Mae and Ugly shared them with neighbors and deer, the next day the trees were full of red apples again.

In their orchard there were always flocks of birds singing their hearts out and eating and feeding their young until the cherries were gone. And the next day the cherry trees were full of cherries again. But Nola Mae was still not happy and never smiled.

In back of the orchard were huge pine trees. Nola Mae had deer feeders attached to them with a picture of deer on a sign. This was much appreciated by the graceful animals. They never strayed to the garden much because the deer feed satisfied them. Once in awhile the apple trees threw apples in their wooded area, which was a special treat for the deer. When neighbors came in the spring, fall, and summer they always left with all kinds of vegetables. Still Nola Mae never smiled.

Meanwhile, Ugly became curious. He hid in a tree one night to see how all of these magical things were happening. Just as Ugly dozed off and fell out of the tree to the ground, a funny looking little man with a green leaf head was holding his tummy laughing. His legs were tree stumps, and his arms and hands were limbs. He said in between chuckles, "I am Dryad a wood nymph whose home is in this garden. You are trespassing."

Ugly squawked, then he screeched. He grabbed Dryad with his beak by his green leaf hair lifting him off the ground. "You are the one who is trespassing. This is Nola Mae's garden. Everyone has wondered why our garden never ran out of fruits or vegetables. Do you know the answer?"

Dryad was angry. His face turned red as a beet. He wiggled trying to get loose from Ugly's big beak. "Oh alas! Of course I know the secret. Let me go you big gook! If you don't let me go when daylight appears, you, Nola Mae and me will be turned into big boulders. The magic of the garden will disappear and be full of dead weeds, and will never be a growing magical garden again."

Ugly said, "Okay Dryad, I will hold you in my claws until you tell me the secret of the garden! After you tell me the secret I will let you go."

With a mischievous smile Dryad said, "You promise Ugly?"

"I promise Dryad."

Dryad said, "A Nymph never goes back on his word. Listen to me. And with a glassy stare at Ugly he began this tale.

"Trees furnish food with shade for the garden. Dew that falls from the trees onto the earth is called honeydew. It is magical food for fairies, elves and nymphs and everything that grows in the garden. The grass where we are standing is called a fairy ring. An unfriendly elf could cause mysterious illness or even death. One never sees him, so if you don't keep your word Ugly, you will not live with Nola Mae on Pryor Mountain again, because you both will be stone dead."

Then in a weird voice he began this tale. "We knew Hunter kidnapped Nola Mae. The fairies, elves, and nymphs decided to help and care for her until she returns to Pryor Mountain where you and Nola Mae will smile and be young again! That is the secret, and if you tell, so sad, too bad!"

The moon was very bright, and as Ugly looked at it, he saw that it was not the moon. It was the Eye Book with its roving eye watching them. Seeing this, Ugly's parrot mouth flew open and he dropped Dyrad.

When this happened, Dyrad took advantage of Ugly and threw Honey Dew in Ugly's face, saying in Nymph tongue, "Now you won't wake up until the morning."

While Ugly was sleeping, the bright sun woke him up. Dyrad had left before daylight.

A voice echoed through the woods calling for Ugly. It was Nola Mae.

Ugly called back saying, "I'm here Nola Mae. I've been in a deep sleep." He flew and perched on her shoulder.

In the distance stood the Golden Buck. A booming voice called out saying "Mount me Nola Mae and Ugly. This has all been a nightmare. You have been asleep Ugly. You or Nola Mae will remember nothing."

Nola Mae and Ugly were in their little cave mountain house on Pryor Mountain again. Nola Mae was smiling and laughing.

Ugly said, "You are so beautiful Nola Mae."

Nola Mae with the Eye Book in her lap smiled and said "What I know." She gently stroked his feathers, as she said, "And you are so handsome Ugly."

The Eye Book was smiling too as it closed its roving eye. It had been a night that no one would remember!

# The Three Little Monkeys

*Grandpa would be happy that I remember him and the 'Three Little Monkeys gift he gave me. I still have them and have never forgotten their messages.*

I still remember our beautiful old Victorian house sitting on a hill with steep steps leading up to the front porch with that wonderful swing. It was the early 40's and the streets were vacant, maybe a car now and then or a bicycle whizzing by. This one particular afternoon, my mother came running out the front door, yanking me from the swing whispering "Sh!" She pulled me through the door. "Be quiet child," she said as she peeked behind the curtains. I looked too. I knew what was happening. There was my little Grandpa staggering down the street and up the steps of our house. Oops, he wobbled and fell back down the steps. "Oh I hope the neighbors aren't watching," Mama whispered. I had to cover my mouth with my hand to stifle a snicker.

Our good Italian neighbors, the Montana's who lived across the street, never missed seeing or hearing a thing that went on in our neighborhood. I just knew they were peering out their windows laughing. Finally Grandpa made it up the steps to our porch. He rang our doorbell. We could hear him mumbling. "They're home. They're just ashamed of me." Then he popped himself in the swing singing songs and finally dozing off. Grandpa didn't live with us, but we kept a room for him when he decided to visit. Papa and Mama didn't have any kind of the devil drink in our house that Grandpa drank at the corner tavern. He had five grown children and he took turns living with them. It just depended on his mood, and right now he was keeping us prisoners until his son, my dad, came home and straightened him out with a cold shower. After that mama fixed him some hot tea. Grandpa was happy-go-lucky whom everyone loved. Later in my adult life, I realized that way back then it was a meeting place for the elderly men to meet their friends and have a few beers. I loved him no matter what. In fact he reminded me of Popeye the Sailor Man. He was muscular and very limber. He could outwrestle the young dudes as well as his elderly friends. And no one could outwalk him. He didn't have a car, which was not unusual for this day, so he walked everywhere. His friends called him Hank. I liked his round, pink cheeks, his twinkling blue eyes, and his chuckling. He always had a chaw of tobacco in his mouth. Mama reluctantly kept a spittoon in his room. He could spit further than anyone I had ever seen and never missed the pot. As I watched him accomplish this feat, I stood in awe.

But that's not all my Grandpa could do. Grandpa could charm warts off of anyone. My girlfriend, Boots, had an ugly protruding wart on the corner of her mouth. Someone told her that if she took her mother's dishcloth and buried it by the light of the moon it would go away. But that did not work. She had been to every doctor in town to make it disappear, but no luck. I told her Mama one-day that my Grandpa could charm the wart off. She just laughed as she said, "You are so funny Chas, what an imagination you have!"

One day I sneaked Boots into my Grandpa's room. "Grandpa, I said, "Please charm that wart off Boots's mouth." She trembled, as he pulled her to him, looking at the ugly thing. He stuck his finger into his mouth bringing a little tabacco juice out on his finger and touched that wart saying some words that we couldn't understand. Then with a twinkle in those blue eyes, he let Boots go with a slap on her fanny and said, "Don't think about this wart going away. Just forget about it."

I'll never forget the sick look on Boots' face as she ran out of his room, wiping the juice from her wart with the back of her hand. Grandpa just chuckled. Well, from that day on, Boots or her mother would wisecrack, "You can see that it's still there, Chas. Where are your Grandpa's, magic powers?"

I was taught always to be polite, but I couldn't let her make fun of my Grandpa's powers that way, so I'd say in a firm voice, "No, I don't expect it will ever go away, cause you're not going to ever stop talking' about it." After that remark from me, they stopped talking about it to me.

One morning I stopped by to get Boots who was still eating her breakfast for school. I said, "You look different this morning Boots. Are you sick?"

Her mother peered over at her. She shrieked, knocking her coffee over. She bolted from the room screaming hysterically, "It's gone! It's gone!" She quickly returned with a mirror in her hand and shoved it in Boots's bewildered face. "Your wart is gone darling." Looking at me, as if I was a high priestess, she said, "Your Grandpa charmed it away." That day, my Grandpa was a hero. Everyone in the neighborhood heard about it. They offered Grandpa money if he would tell his secret. He said, "If I take money or tell anyone how it's done, I will lose the gift." I was so proud of him. From that day on, if anyone had a wart, they came to my loveable hero Grandpa.

One day, hand in hand, Grandpa and I walked to Happy Hollow Park, which he and my Grandma that I never knew used to own. He would tell me stories how his family enjoyed living in Happy Hollow where nature and animals surrounded them. This particular day we sat down on a rickety bench, me cuddling up to his side, talking about fishing, which we loved to do together. He reached deep into his pants pocket and brought out three funny looking little ivory monkeys. They were attached together. He said, "Here's a little gift for you sweetheart." Now Grandpa never gave me anything in my whole life, except his love. I looked at these weird monkeys closely, rubbing my fingers over their smooth ivory coating. I asked, "What are they doing Grandpa?"

Grandpa began to explain, as he pointed to the first one. "This one is covering his eyes, and he is saying, "See no evil." Then he put his finger on the second little monkey who was covering his ears and said, "Hear no evil." Then he said, "The third little monkey is saying, "Speak no evil." This was the most memorable moment with my Grandpa I ever had. All through life I never forgot the little monkey's messages. What an unexpected lesson I learned that day.

That night Grandpa left our house and was killed. Later I heard he went down to the corner tavern to shoot the bull with his friends and drank a couple of snowcapped beers. On the way back to our house he stepped into a path of a car and was killed instantly. Mama and Papa wouldn't let me go to his funeral. They said, "Grandpa would want you to remember him as he was."

The day of his funeral, I stayed with my friend Boots, who was just as sad as I was about him not being around anymore. We went to Happy Hollow and sat on the rickety bench looking at the monkeys he had given me. Boots and I didn't talk much that day. When we started to leave, I stepped into a juicy chaw of tobacco. As the wind blew by, we thought we heard a low chuckle.

# The Lonesome Old Man

*This story won an award at a writing conference
It also was published in a magazine.*

By Chastine Ellen Shumway

RG was an old man who lived by himself in a trailer in the Ozark Mountains. Although this man was old and limped because of an injury in the war, he was very strong. He chopped down trees and cut them into pieces to heat his trailer in the winter. He sold wood to his neighbors. In the evening he played tunes on his harmonica. He did not have a wife. He did not have any children. All he had were chickens and two baby squirrels. RG was lonesome. One morning he heard a commotion in his back yard. His chickens were cackling loudly. He grabbed his gun and ran out the door. There was a little black and tan dog chasing his chickens. Most people shot dogs when they chased chickens. RG had a kind heart. He laid his gun down. He caught the little dog and held him at arm's length. The dog wiggled. He tried to get loose. RG hugged him close to his chest. The little dog licked RG's face. With a big grin on his face, the old man said, "Why little fellow, you like me." RG limped over to his pickup truck and put the little dog on the seat. RG said, "A nice little dog like you surely belongs to someone. Let's go look for your family." They drove over the big mountains. They drove through a forest of tall pine trees until they came to a small town. RG asked everyone he saw if they knew who the little dog belonged to. No one knew. It was growing dark. The little dog cuddled up to RG as they drove home. I'm going to name you JR, my new friend. RG was so happy he sang all the way back to his trailer. JR howled as he tried to sing too. Then JR fell fast asleep. RG carried him to his bedroom and laid him on a soft pillow at the foot of his bed. He said his prayers and thanked God for JR. The next morning when the old man woke up, JR was snoring.

RG and JR ate breakfast together. Then they went outside. The chickens were scratching and pecking for little bugs that lived in the ground. JR began chasing the chickens.

RG hollered, "No JR!" The little dog minded him. "Good dog!" RG patted him on the head. He showed JR his two squirrels. JR barked. The squirrels barked back at him. RG went into the woods. JR followed him. He got his buzz saw out and began splitting wood. Then he took a small piece of wood and threw it in to the air. JR caught it in midair. "Good Dog, you are smart." RG rewarded him with a dog biscuit. The old man was happier than he had ever been.

One day Fuzz, a new neighborhood Angora cat came over to play with JR. A big dog called Bruiser saw they were having so much fun, he decided to join them. His bark startled Fuzz. She tore off running with her fuzzy tail high in the air. Bruiser ran faster. He grabbed Fuzzies tail pulling a mouth of fur out. She let out a big meow and escaped to a big pine tree running up it as fast as she could. Ms. Burnett, a widow woman who owned Fuzz saw what was happening. She grabbed her broom and ran out of the house screaming. She whacked Bruiser over the head. He ran away yelping. The widow tried to coax Fuzz down, but Fuzz had ventured too far up the tree.

The commotion echoed to RG's trailer. RG had not met his neighbor. He hopped on his four-wheeler and bounced over the rocky road to the tree. He scolded JR. The little dog acted ashamed. The wind began blowing. The limbs of the big pine tree swayed back and forth with Fuzz holding on and mewing with fear.

Someone called the fire department. Sirens screamed throughout the mountains. A firewoman called Missy jumped out of the red fire truck. First she tried to coax Fuzz down with a can of tuna. That did not work. Missy got an extension ladder and put it against the tall tree. Missy climbed up the ladder until she could climb no more. The ladder was not long enough. She called the Mayor on her cell phone. The Mayor came out to see how the problem could be solved. The sky grew dark, and the wind began to blow harder. Big drops of rain began falling. The Mayor said, "There's a storm brewing. We'll have to wait until it blows over and then rescue the cat." Tears rolled down Ms. Burnett's wrinkled face.

Without warning RG jumped off of his four wheeler. He limped fast over to the tree. Before anyone could stop him he swung up on the rungs of the ladder like a monkey. He climbed until there were no more rungs to climb. He grabbed a strong looking branch of the tree and pulled himself up into the branches. The cat's tail was hanging just a hair away from RG's hand. Quickly he grabbed Fuzzies tail. She screamed like a banshee, MEOWWWWWWWWWWWWWWWWW! RG cradled the wiggling cat under one arm. When they got on the ground, RG handed the cat to Ms. Burnett and said, "I'm sorry my dog JR chased your cat up the tree."

As she hugged him she said, "Your dog didn't chase my cat. It was another dog. You and your dog are heroes!' She hugged him. Then she gave him freshly baked cookies. RG picked JR up and said, "Good dog!" When they got home, they sat on the porch together with JR eating some dog bones and RG eating cookies with coffee. Then RG happily played the harmonica while JR howled. Theirs was a happy life, because they found each other and became good friends.

# Delta Black Boy's Adventure

By Chastine Ellen Shumway

Mama stood in the doorway of the unpainted wooden shack calling, "Curtis". Wiping her hands on her feed sack apron she said aloud, "Laudy, All Mighty, where is dat youngun gone to now?"

A burr headed, barefoot boy came running round the house with a burlap feed sack swinging from his shoulder. "Gonna find Prissy, mama. Dat cat been gone too long."

His mama nodded her head, saying, "Uh, uh! Well don't go near the kudzu bottoms. De bogeyman might ketch you. If Prissy's in there, she's gone for good." The morning sun was already hot. She stopped talking as she lifted her apron mopping the sweat trickling down her face. "Before ya go, git your Pa out of the cotton field for lunch. Ya hear?"

"Yasum mama." Curtis licked his chops. The scent was drifting through the air of fat bacon, beans, cornbread, wild honey, and fried onions.

Curtis knew about that kudzu too. It was a creepy, green monstrous crawling vine, a complete destruction of any living thing in its path. It smothered its victims under sun-craving leaves. "Don't worry mama, I'll be careful." The thought of Prissy being caught by the choking kudzu vines made him shiver. As he danced down the road, he kicked a pebble now and then to see how far it would go. "Here Prissy, here Prissy, where's you hidin yer yallar face?" He licked the salty sweat that trickled down his ebony face. Soon he came to a field where his Pa was plowing with his stubborn mules, Jake and Luweezy. Calling out to him, he said, "Mama says lunch will be ready soon, Pa."

"Whoa Jake. Whoa, Luweezy, Whoa!" Every muscle in his father's strong black arms rippled as he pulled the mules to a stop. "Where ya headed son?"

"Looking for Prissy. She's sho nuff run away, but I'se be home before dark, Pa. Make sure mama saves some of those vittles fer me." Curtis quickened his pace. Thinking about that good food was making his mouth water. As he rounded the bend he started walking in the middle of the road. He was dreading the encounter with the mysterious kudzu vines. If Prissy were tangled in it, he would have to figure out a way to save her. It was the talk of the Delta that the bugaboo man lived in its depths. At night, the bugaboo man wandered around looking for trespassers, man or beast. Mama told him stories about how Brer Rabbit outsmarted the bugaboo man though.

EEEEEEEE! A blood-curdling scream ripped through the silence of the Delta. Curtis froze in terror. Fear pricked at the base of his spine. His eyes bugged out. He shook so hard, his teeth rattled. Then he heard a deafening thunder of a voice. "I've got you varmints now."

Curtis fell to the ground and crawled through the tall grass like the snakes he watched slithering around at the river. Then he heard a loud, persistent plaintive meowing. He parted the tall grass ever so quietly. His eyes bugged out. There stood gruff Old Man Tate, the man his parents worked for with his arms full of kittens. Prissy had new babies! One at a time, he was putting them into a wooden crate.

Just then, screeching like a banshee, her yallar fur electrified in all directions, Prissy somersaulted off the barn with her sharp claws spread out for action. She landed on Old Man Tate's head, her claws raking and gashing his forehead. His hand swung up to grab her. Missing her, he held a hand full of fur. Prissy leaped to the ground, dropped on all four feet and took off running.

"That darn cat!" Old Man Tate muttered. Then jerking his red bandana from his hip pocket he wiped the blood off his forehead. "You're too late mama cat, I'm taking your troublesome babies far away." Just then, his beady eyes discovered Curtis, hiding. "I see ya boy. Get your behind back to your Pa's and help him with the work that I pay your family to do. You don't have any business dilly-dallying around in these parts no how."

Curtis jumped from his hiding place. With his head bent low like a billygoat and his fists clenched tightly aimed them towards Old Man Tate's fat pouch of a belly. He yelled, "You leave Prissy and her babies alone."

Old Man Tate grabbed Curtis by his overall straps. He picked him up off the ground and held him high in the air. Curtis' arms and legs were dancing. "You big bully, put me down. Put me down."

"Don't talk to me like that, boy. Where's your respect?" Out of nowhere, Prissy crossed between Old Man Tate's feet tripping him and causing him to lose his balance. He spun on his heels and stumbled backwards and plunged against the barn with a loud thud loosing his grip on Curtis. Curtis sailed through the air, as floundering Old Man Tate fell to the ground. Curtis was free!

"Thanks Prissy. Hurry! We've got to get away from here! Feet do yo stuff, we're headin' home!"

But Prissy had disappeared. Curtis' stomach began to feel queasy. Then a noisy rustling came from a clump of weeds. Out walked a proud

Prissy holding a tiny bundle of fur in her mouth. Prissy nudged Curtis' leg affectionately. Walking closer to the weeds, Curtis prodded the greenery with his foot. Out came two more kittens purring. In the entire racket, Prissy had saved and hidden her babies.

Old Man Tate was slowly getting back on his feet. Through all of the commotion the feed sack was still on Curtis' back that he had brought. Stooping down, Curtis grabbed Prissy by the back of her neck and crammed her into it. He snatched the babies up and threw them in too. Then he hollered, "Feet do yo stuff!" He slung the burlap bag full of kittens over his shoulder and broke into a wild run.

Watching him go, Tate spat a stream of brown tobacco juice from his mouth. Then he doubled over laughing. He said, "That boy sure loves that yallar cat. And that mama cat sure loved my chickens"

The day, which had been so bright and sunny was being blanketed by the shadows of night. It was way past suppertime. Curtis ran without looking back until he felt his insides would fall out. His sides ached with sharp pains. As he rounded the bend, he saw his Mama and Papa standing on the porch. What a glorious sight! He breathed a deep sigh of relief as he bolted up the steps and fell against his mama's breast, panting and drawing in deep breaths of air. "Where have you been sugar?" Mama asked, as she cuddled him in her arms hugging him against her breast.

His father said, "Your shirt is torn and muddy, son. What happened?" Curtis handed him the gunnysack. Prissy and her younguns sprinted out.

His mama said, "I've kept your food warm on the stove. You need to eat and rest before you tell us where you found Prissy and her kittens. She led him to the table, and heaped his plate full of black-eyed peas and cornbread.

Curtis slurped the beans down, dipping the hot buttered cornbread into their thick juice. He licked his lips catching the drippings. "Mama dem beans are sho good!" She hugged him and gave him some sugar cookies she had baked. Prissy was lapping a big bowl of warm milk, while the baby kittens purred contentedly as they nursed on her. In between bites of food, Curtis told his Mama and Papa about the rescue of Prissy and her kittens..

When Curtis finished talking and eating. Mama said, "You've had a trying day. It's time for you and Prissy to go to bed. Let's say a prayer for Old Man Tate. Papa will talk to him tomorrow."

Curtis grinned broadly, and Prissy purred contentedly. They were not afraid anymore. With their bellies full and the warmth of Mama and Papa's love and soft voices filling the room, they soon drifted off to dreamland on Curtis' wonderful bed with the corn-shuck filled mattress.

# Delta Black Boy And Big Ole Kat

By Chastine Ellen Shumway

Big Kat

Curtis woke to the tinkling of the rain on the tin roof of their shanty. He wiggled his toes. He was excited because the annual fall church picnic was coming. It was always on the first Sunday in October. It was a gladsome event that engulfed the 100-year-old Baptist Church in Mississippi. A muffled meow rang out from under the covers. It was his faithful cat and constant companion, Prissy. She kept his feet warm at night with her yallar fur. Curtis kicked the covers off of his feet. Prissy jumped off his bed meowing in fierce resentment of being bothered. Her fur was electrified and stood on end. Prissy was angry because she had been dreaming about catching a juicy mouse. As usual her master had to wake her up with his wiggling toes. Curtis crawled out of bed. Then he stooped down looking under his bed where Prissy had crawled.

In a pleading voice, he said, "Ahhh come on out Prissy. Don't be mad at me. I'se got plans for you and me today. We're goin' fishin'. The fish love rainy days, and they will be jumpin' in the air and bitin' well today. We're gwine to try and catch big Ole Kat so the church picnic will have enough fish to fill every ones bellies."

Now Ole Kat was not just any fish, mind you. He was a 43'inch long 50-pound flathead catfish who had outsmarted the best of fishermen in the Delta. All of a sudden Prissy came out from under the bed. She hunched her body with her fur electrified. Her green eyes glowed with determination. She saw something! A large cockroach raced across the slatted floor. Prissy pounced on it and began toying with it. Curtis laughed as he slipped on his patched jeans and took the roach from Prissy's paws and put it in his cardboard tackle box. Curtis had never heard of anyone ever feeding Ole Kat a juicy roach. He said to Prissy, "Ole Kat has grown bigger and bigger and will feed lots of people. We have to catch him!" All of a sudden he closed his eyes and took a deep breath, smelling the aroma of bacon and hot biscuits covered with home churned butter and sorghum cooking in the kitchen. With Prissy at his heels, they raced into the kitchen.

Mama greeted them with some milk coffee and poured some milk into Prissy's bowl. It was her day to do ironing for Mizz Ellie at de big house. His mama took off her apron and gave him a big hug as she walked out the door, saying, "Don't fergit to do your chores before you go fishin' son."

Curtis grumbled a little under his breath, as he pocketed the leftover biscuits that he and his friend Simmons would eat while fishing. He knew that there was no way he could crawfish out of his duties. If he didn't have his chores done when mama got back, his Pa would use the hickory switch on his rump. His thoughts went back to the picnic. He had helped pick green beans, black-eyed peas, butter beans, cucumbers, potatoes and tomatoes from their huge garden. One morning he was watching his mama and his granny shell the butterbeans. They were talking about things that didn't usually interest him. All of a sudden his ears perked up when he heard his granny saying that there was going to be a problem at the picnic. She said, "It will be the first time that noone has caught enough fish in the history of the annual picnic to feed the upcoming crowd." Curtis made up his mind right there and then that he and his best friend Simmons would go fishin' and catch Ole Kat to have enough fish for the picnic. He licked his chops as he thought of the large bowls of vegetables and the platters heaped with fried chicken and fish fried right there in the big black frying pan. To go with that there were wicker baskets filled with cornbread, rolls and other biscuits on the picnic tables. The best part of the picnic lunch was lots of coolers of homemade ice cream. After filling their bellies there was always a sack race. The game included an old empty gunnysack which chicken feed came in. There were two kids for each sack. Each one would put one leg in the sack. Then they would hold their side of the sack with one hand and their other foot outside the sack and run for the finish line. The prize was a Bible to the winners. Curtis and Simmons practiced the race almost everyday for this big event.

The girls had a potato contest seeing who could peel the longest skin off of a potato without breaking it. The longest skin won the prize.

Back to his thoughts of going fishing, Curtis called "Come on Prissy, let's git my fishin' pole off the back porch." Curtis was proud of his pole. It was a cane pole with string and a homemade pin hook attached. While he fed the chickens, Prissy, with her neck hair electrified chased Cocky, the rooster, as they ran down the dusty dirt road.

They passed the big house where mama worked. It was a beautiful Southern Mansion with swaying moss on loblolly trees lining a circular drive. Simmons lived there. Curtis cupped his mouth with his hands, and in a shrill voice called three catbird calls. The front door of the house opened, and out ran a boy with red hair and lots of freckles carrying a pole. "Hi Curt, your mama told me you were going fishing today. Knowing we are fishing buddies, I knew you'd be by soon."

"Yeah Simmons, I knew mama would tell you I wuz comin' by. It's a good rainy day to catch Big Kat and have enough fish for the picnic."

They passed several tenant shanties like the one Curtis lived in, on the way to the river. Some people were sitting on their front porches in wicker rockers enjoying the pinging sound of rain on their tin roof. They waved at the boys as they passed by. It wasn't long before Curtis and Simmons reached the Little Red River with Prissy following at their heels.

As they sat down under the welcomed Willow Tree, with its protective vining limbs, Simmons chuckled and said, "Spit on your hook for good luck Curt." Both boys spit on their hooks.

Simmons said, "We'll need all the help we can get to catch big ole Kat! Where's the bait?"

As Curt lifted the lid carefully, he said, "This is our piece of good luck." The cockroach was limp, his whiskers barely twitching.

Simmons eyes bugged out. "Jeez Curt, whoever heard of a roach for bait?"

Curt snickered saying, "Well Prissy caught it this morning, and I reckoned we should use it for bait. It might change our luck."

Both boys threw their fish lines in the water. All of a sudden, Curtis felt a jerk on his hook. He jumped up seeing a monstrous fish in about 2 feet of water chasing after the now lively wiggling roach. With one big gulp, big Kat nipped at the roach. Now the line was tangled all around Big Kat. Then the line broke.

Simmons screamed, his voice echoing through the woods. "Don't lose that sly Ole Kat Curtis. We need to jump into the water or we will lose him." With that statement he jumped into the water, clothes and all, where the fish was struggling and flopping. He grabbed a gill. Curt jumped into the water and grabbed the other gill. The battle was on! The boys held on to the gills and struggled with Ole Kat. People hearing the racket from afar started running to the river. The fish was fighting and both the boys kept holding on to the gills for dear life. The fish was so big, it took both boys all over and under the water. The battle lasted for a long time. When it was over both boys were exhausted, including the fish, which had to be hauled fifteen feet up the bank. The boys were wet and tired. Curtis' mom and Simmons mom heard the commotion of the rooting crowd and were there with blankets to wrap around them. Looking at the huge fish, Curtis said, "Sho nuff it was all worth it. You don't get a chance to catch a fish like Big Kat very often."

Simmons replied, "Yeah man, you're right!"

Now the men of the church had the big job of preparing Big Ole Kat for the women to work on. The boys watched them, and so did Prissy, as the men were opening Kat's fat belly. They knew that as old and big as Kat was that he would have lots of things in his belly, because catfish are scavengers that moved only when food was near. When the men slit Kat's big belly all sorts of debris spilled on the tailgate of one of the men's truck. The boys eyes were big as a saucer when they saw a spark plug, a marble, lots of half eaten minnows and small fish, two pennies and human waste.

Simmons with his freckles standing out said, "Curtis, I can't believe that we caught Big Kat!

Two muscle bound men hoisted the boys on their shoulders with the crowd cheering.

The annual church picnic was a big success with plenty of fish and chicken. The men who cleaned Big Kat said they were amazed when they opened big Kat up and saw all of the junk he had eaten.

It was lots of work, and as the moon broke through the scattered clouds, one of the men said to Curt and Simmons, "Okay Champion Fishermen, it's past your bedtime. I'll take you home."

Prissy didn't want to leave, as she had her belly filled with the half-eaten minnows and pieces of the fish. She rubbed her fur against Curtis' leg, purring softly. She was in cat heaven. The churchwomen had their work cut out for them the following week at the church.

The day of the picnic finally arrived. Curtis was scrubbed until his black skin shined like a silver dollar. His friend Simmons was slicked up too. He was smiling and showed his buckteeth. They and their other friends helped set up the tables while the ladies put the homemade food on them, which was enough to feed the whole state of Mississippi and desserts to die for. There were large bowls of vegetables, platters of chicken and fish, lemonade and iced tea. The aroma of homemade yeast and corn rolls and biscuits filled the air. Everyone looked forward to the dessert, which was gallons of ice cream, all kinds of cookies, pies and cakes.

After everyone had eaten, the games began for the children. The favorite game was the sack race. The girls looked forward to the potato game. The girl who peeled the longest potato skin without it breaking would win. Lucy, (unbeknownst to anyone that she was Curtis' girlfriend) won that race. Curtis and Simmons won the sack race and were given the Bibles. It was a day worth waiting for, but Curtis and Simmons were a little sad, that Big Kat was finally caught.

# Zophana, The Colorful Man

By My Granddaughter, Maria Brummett

The colorful man paraded down the street showing the customs of his country Zimbabwe

His family supported him from the crowd, cheering him on. His name was Zophana. The sun was blazing down on him making him look shinny but it was just the sweat rolling down his ebony face. The sun was not going to ruin Zophana's parade. Zophana was having the best time. He does not care what people think about him since he is a different color because he knows that God loves him and in God's eyes everyone is the same color. He always loves to show pride for his country. Zophana also has another advantage besides being in the parade. He is turning 38. Once the parade ends, he's going to a festival with his family, not knowing what's going to happen. The last present came to be opened, but the strange thing about the present was an enclosed card. During the parade he made a friend with a man called Steve who lived in the United States. Steve was rich and Steve and Zophana became great friends. Steve found out how poor Zophana and his family was. He felt sorry for him. Zophana invited Steve to the festival and told him where it was. Steve could not be there. Without anyone knowing it, Steve went home and went to the festival before anyone was there. Zophana opened the last present and inside was lots of money and four airplane tickets back to his home and then to the U. S. A. Zophana thought who would be so generous to do this. Once he got back to his home in Africa he packed up and went back to the U.S.A. He looked up Steve but didn't know Steve's last name. But then he remembered Steve's nametag. It said Steve McNice. He looked him up and thanked him. Now Zophana and Steven are good friends.

# Rolling With The Punches

*This Story appeared in The Good Old Days magazine. May, 2000*

By Chastine Ellen Shumway

Mama dear, how I miss you! I was so lucky that God loaned you to me. Why I can remember way back when I just started to school at that one-room schoolhouse in Ohio. I was so excited! I wore my little red plaid dress with the sailor collar and bow that your hands so lovingly made for me.

Everything went well at school that first morning, that is, until recess. The girls and I were picking dandelions and smashing them with a brick, pretending we were nurses making medicine. Then I hit my thumb.

I tore off through the grassy commons down the path toward home. I could hear the school bell clanging, calling me to come back, but my legs just ran faster to the safe place, home. I dashed through the front door, and there stood my beautiful mama in her cobbler apron. A surprised look covered her face and then she broke into a radiant smile. I threw my arms around her, sobbing like my heart would break. She wiped the tears from my swollen face with her apron, soothing me, as I blurted out what had happened.

She didn't scold me. She led me to the bathroom, and ran cold water over my sore thumb. Then she wrapped it in gauze. Then she picked me up and carried me to the creaky hickory rocking chair and rocked me to sleep.

The next day, written excuse in hand, I returned to school. I marched into the classroom and handed the note to bespectacled Ms. Beckett. Recess came again. Things didn't turn out like I wanted so I headed home again. Mama met me with a perplexed look, but I knew she was happy to see me. I stayed home the rest of the day.

The next morning, excuse in hand, I walked into class. Ms. Beckett didn't have a happy face when she looked over her glasses at me with a stony glare. It made me feel a little self-conscious. By the time recess came, I was depressed. When Sarah wouldn't let me jump the rope, I pouted. Some of the little girl classmates yelled, "Why don't you run home again, Chastine?" Well, I didn't disappoint them. I kicked up my heels and headed down the worn path towards home. Mama was standing at the door this time like she was expecting me. She had a note in her hand. Wiping my tears away, she fixed me a cup of cocoa, but there was something different today.

With a shaky voice and teary eyes, she said, "Darlin', you need to go back to school now so you will grow up to be a smart young lady."

I took the note from her hand, knowing everything would be all right. When I got to the little one-room schoolhouse everything was quiet. Ms. Beckett was not at her desk. She was sitting in a circle surrounded by the students, who were reading books. She didn't look up. There was one empty chair in the circle next to Ms. Beckett. Mine I thought. But first I had to give the magic note to her. I strutted up to the teacher and stretched my arm out handing her the note that would solve my problems. But before I could turn and go to my seat, she snatched my arm and jerked me across her lap. She gave me a few resounding slaps on my fanny. I made up my mind not to cry, but I was mortified. As I quickly went to my seat, I heard a few smothered snickers.

I grew up that day from Mama's little spoiled girl. That night I heard Mama telling Papa how she hated cutting the apron strings, but it had to be done. I really didn't understand what she meant, but I know now.

Looking back on my life, I've wanted to run away from life from time to time, but then I see a little girl being paddled for running away.

The memory makes me laugh, but I learned the lesson well. You have to roll with the punches that comes with life, and no matter how tough life gets, you've got to hang in there!

# Ozark Recollections

*Memories are made of this. Part of this story is true. To this day, both brothers, Dick and Art are still close. The author is proud that our family is known as a close family.*
*Dick was the oldest. When he went into the service, he gave Art his sharp looking car and his motorcycle, which made Artie very popular at his school.*

Our grandfather Bompie was about 65 years old when I was a boy of 12. You couldn't tell he was old unless you looked at his weathered beaten face. He had rock like arms. He reminded us of Popeye the Sailor Man, 'cause he could win in arm wrestling with anyone who challenged him. He never said much, just a "Maybe," or "You don't say," or "Reckon so," or "If God's willing." He was always cheerful with a ready smile for everyone. What us six kids loved about him was his 'can do' spirit and his love of GOD, his family, and the Ozarks. We learned from him that if a man's word wasn't good, then the man wasn't worth much. He always had time for my older brother, Dick and me, no matter how busy he was. If we asked him if he thought we could do something, he would reply, You can do anything if you make up your mind to. Just follow your dreams.

Bompie served in World War 1. We learned that our Bompie was a gutsy man. When he was on a ship in the Navy a long time ago, he heard his mother was dying with cancer. He couldn't get permission to go home, so he jumped off the ship and was swimming to shore to go to her. Of course he was caught, and was on bread and water for awhile. Later on he was discharged from the U. S. Navy, because he had a heart ailment.

My Grandmother, (we called her Mom), worried about him, but he would just say to her, "Baby Doll, there's nothing wrong with me that a kiss won't cure." Then he kissed her on the cheek, and sometimes patted her on the fanny. We six kids just hooted when her chubby cheeks grew pink. We called her Mom ever since we were younguns. I don't remember why, nor could anyone else figure that out. She was sort of big, but when she complained about being big, we would throw our arms around her and say, "We like big Moms." She looked like a Grandma should look with her white hair pulled back into a bun, and she had a large free-swinging bosom. She usually wore a neat looking cobbler apron, cause it seemed she was always in the kitchen stirring up goodies to eat for our large brood. It felt so good when we leaned our heads against her breast when she rocked us when we were small. But what we really remember about our Mom was the smell of cinnamon and sugar donuts drifting through the air as we got off the school bus. We'd race up the hill into the house trying to be the first kid through the door and into the kitchen. Bompie would be sitting at the table with steaming coffee dunking his donuts. A big pitcher of cold milk awaited us with a heaping plate of rolls and donuts. We sat down and joined the Dunker's Club. We welcomed the weekends when there wasn't any school for a couple of days. In the evenings our Mama would go to the piano in the parlor and play our favorite songs while we sang. Then we nibbled on chocolate fudge, or Bompie would get the longhandled popcorn popper and pop corn in the fireplace.

In our front yard stood a huge oak tree with a tire hanging by strong hemp ropes from its staunch branches. We kids would swing, one by one, until the cat would die. I can still smell that hemp rope and feel its rough texture on my hands. Sometimes I would get a rope burn, but I wiped my sweaty hands on my patched jeans and got on with living. This place was a heaven on earth to us kids.

We had about 40 acres covered with wall to wall towering pine trees. We never had to buy Christmas trees. There was also a spring fed creek that bordered our land. It had lots of sunfish in it. When my brother Dick, our buddies and me went fishing, we spit on the hook for good luck. We called the stream, 'Crazy Creek' cause there were black round rocks in it with a bubbling spring splashing over them. Many a time I would cup my hands catching the cool water and hurriedly raising it to my mouth slurping it quickly before it slid through my fingers. Walking along the banks of the creek that cut through our property was our favorite part of our land. In the evening the bullfrogs went crazy with their croaking orchestras. The geese honked as they formed a v-shape formation flying through the air to bed in for the night.

We had a garden, which my brother and I tended. Our pantry was always stocked full of canned goods. Did you ever smell the wonderful aroma of a tomato hanging on the vine? The taste is wonderful. We'd pick a tomato, spit on it and wipe the dirt from it on our pants, and take a juicy bite from it. Now there's no taste like a ripe red tomato with the juice trickling down your chin. I guess the flavor comes from the good old Ozark Mountain soil. Until my sisters grew up, they thought that butter beans had real butter inside of them. But to me and everyone else in our family, I s'pose, we couldn't wait for the Blue Kentucky green beans to be ready to pick. I called them 'The First Pickins.' With large gunnysacks in our hands, my brother Dick and me would head to the garden and carefully pick those green beans. When we got our first sack full, I would run in the house panting and calling "Mama here is the first 'pickins' of green beans." That night my four sisters, Sandy, Susie, Florence and Betty sat with Mom and Mama in the big kitchen at the round oak table snapping the beans. First the ends were pinched off. Then they were broken into 3 pieces and put into a huge pot with a piece of jowl and onions and cooked slowly until the next day. My saliva is working right now as I recall the aroma and taste of the 'First Pickins.'

Our Pa Wil was a truck driver, and we didn't see much of him. I guess that is why Bompie, my Brother Dick, and I were so close. Mama said, "These three are as close as three peas in a pod"

One day Papa decided we needed some hunting dogs. He knew Bompie loved to hunt and fish. Pa being on the road so much bought two of the sharpest looking beagles in the county for us. We named one beagle, Bad Eye, because he had a circle of black surrounding one eye. Whiskey came by his name, because he found a whiskey bottle one Sunday afternoon on the road. Back then Arkansas was a dry state. Mama had invited the preacher man and his wife for dinner. When everyone came for dinner, Whiskey trotted up with this bottle in his mouth. Mama was humiliated.

Mama was very pretty with her blond hair subdued in a hair net, with ringlets peeking from underneath it. She blushed easily and always had such an angelic face with a Mona Lisa smile. She smelled so good, a sort of clean scented smell. Later after Mama went to heaven, my sisters told me it was cologne called Heaven Scent.

One fall evening before we all went to bed, I could hardly sleep. Bompie said that it was almost time to start preparing our dogs for their first hunt. He said that Little Art (me) would be going too. I was excited as a cricket on a hot tin roof. I couldn't wait for my first hunt. I said, "Bompie how can I go on my first hunt without a gun?"

"He just sort of chuckled, and said, "Artie, things will work out, God willin." That night I didn't sleep at all.

As soon as summer vacation from school started, the three of us would get up every morning at daybreak. We men sat down to a breakfast of pancakes, eggs and sausage mixed with molasses. It was Bompie's specialty. We'd watch Bomp mix this conglomeration up with butter and gooey syrup like we did when we slopped the hogs. We just laughed, but then we tried it, and found that his recipe was sure good eating!

After breakfast, we three musketeers headed to the woods with Whiskey and Bad Eye straining at their leashes and lapping up the air with their tongues. We had a dead rabbit, which we had trapped. While we pulled it around by a string all through the brush, Bompie held the dogs until we had scented the trail. The leaves on the ground crackled as we followed them. The chill of the air was invigorating against our ruddy cheeks. The dogs baying broke the tranquil silence, as they hit a hot trail. Bompie said, "That is the prettiest sound you'll ever hear!"

After the training the dogs started fighting with one another. Bompie swore up and down that they had bulldog in them.

My birthday was coming soon in November. Birthdays were always an important event in our family. It was almost time for the big hunt. I'll never forget that birthday. It was the best! At the breakfast table that crisp fall morning lay a four-ten shotgun from Bompie and Mom. Next to that was a box of shotgun shells from Mama, Pa and the girls. My brother Dick, who by the way, was named after Bomp gave me a pocketknife. My chest swelled and throbbed with pride and emotion, as I shoved the knife deep into the pocket of my blue jeans. I rubbed the smooth handle of the gun. I felt I had become a man at last. It was time for my first hunt.

As we tromped through the Ozark woods, we kicked up a covey of quail, causing them to squawk hysterically and fly into the wide blue yonder. We walked a few steps into an open field. I held my new gun in my hand. Bompie showed me how to load and shoot it. He said, "Son, a gun is dangerous if not handled right. Only kill what you need for the table."

One early morning, we could tell a storm was coming, but we wanted to go hunting before it hit. Not only was it a storm, it turned into a tornado. We found how brave our Bomp was when he covered me with his own body as a funnel black cloud was swooping all around.

Soon it was finally time for the real big hunt. Dick went to get the dogs. The beagles had learned their lessons well. No sooner we got to the woods they were off to the races with their noses sniffing the ground and their tails wagging like a windmill. The hunt was in full gear as the howling dogs hit a trail. All of a sudden a rabbit came running through the brush with the dogs in hot pursuit. As the rabbit circled, I lifted my gun to my shoulder and pulled the trigger. Bam! My gun exploded hitting a little ball of fur.

Bompie said later that my eyes were as big as saucers, but he was proud of me getting it with the first shot. My brother Dick, an experienced hunter, got his limit. We quit hunting in a hurry when Whisky kicked up a skunk. That was quite a scent.

That night we had fried rabbit with mashed potatoes, green beans with hamhocks and cornbread. Mama had made our favorite apple pie with the brown sugar topping. They let me have milkcoffee, while the others drank real coffee.

Papa made it home and was enjoying the conversation about our hunt. I saved the rabbit foot from my first hunt for good luck. I have it to this day.

It wasn't long after our hunts, that Bompie's heart got worse. It became hard for him to go with us on our hunts. We wheeled him out to the woods in a wheelbarrow and kept a comfortable chair under a tree for him covered with blankets. He enjoyed hearing the dog's call of the wild and breathing that good country air.

Now Dick and I have grown up. We have been on many hunts in all parts of the country. We now understand how Bompie felt walking through the Arkansas woods with us long ago. Although he is no longer with us, when the fall arrives with its crisp, chilling air, and we hear the call of the geese flying overhead, we grab our hunting gear and jump in Dick's truck. We are going back to our old home place in Arkansas to God's Country as Bompie called this grand state. And we both agree that there was no hunt like being with Bomp, Dead Eye, and Whiskey.

# An Unbelievable Horse

Written by Chastine Shumway

Illustrated by Joan Waites

*Published by Boy's Quest and bought by SIRS*

*Has won many awards*

The morning dawned brightly. The sun was rising above the mountains bordering the never-ending Plains on June 25, 1876, over 100 years ago. A handsome, proud, spunky, claybrook sorrel gelding, part mustang, with a black mane and tail, weighing about 925 pounds and 15 hands in height, was in battle formation with General Custer and five troops of the Seventh United States Calvary. He was strutting in time with the band playing, "The Girl I left behind." His name was Comanche; he and his owner, Captain Keogh, were riding into battle with General Custer. There was no hint of the bloody scenes that were to make it a memorable, historical day. This would be their last battle. Yes, he was proud to be a part of the U.S. Army with the Seventh Cavalry. This horse was a favorite of the Calvary; the night before the big battle, his soldier buddies played cards. Before settling down for a nap, Keogh gave Comanche a couple of beers, his favorite beverage.

Comanche was purchased by the U.S. Army in 1868 in St. Louis and sent to Fort Leavenworth, Kansas. The minute Captain Myles Keogh saw him, he shelled out $90 to buy him. This was a large sum of money in those days. Captain Keogh used Comanche in all the

Indian skirmishes. He had a special quality of character, combining courage and guts needed for a war-house!

In the fall of 1868, their unit fought the Comanche tribe in Kansas. During the battle, with the Comanche Indians on the Cimarron River, on the Beaver Fork, the horse was wounded in the hip by an arrow. He reared up neighing, but the captain did not realize the horse was injured and continued to fight from his back until the battle was over. Afterward, he discovered an arrow broken off in the horse's rump. The wound was treated. After the horse recovered, he had earned the name Comanche for his bravery in continuing to carry his master despite his own pain.

In a story written by Margaret Leighton, which is reasonably factual, a trooper called McBane said he saw the arrow strike. "He sure squalled as loud as any Comanche. I never heard a horse let out that kind of a holler. A sure enough Comanche yell."

Keogh replied, "Comanche! That's the name for my horse."

Again in 1870, during a battle against the Comanche tribe, he was wounded in battle once more. This time his leg was hurt. He was lame for over a month, but he recovered.

Then in 1871, Comanche was wounded in battle once more; this time the wound was in his shoulder. Once again, he recovered quickly. The cavalry was very proud of this tough, fearless, soldierly horse that continued to go into battle despite being wounded so many times.

On June 25, 1876, the cavalry was headed into another battle. It would be their last battle, The Battle of the Bighorn. The Little Bighorn River flowed to the north; its shallow winding courses were marked by clumps of the stately cottonwood timbers. Deep ravines rose steeply from the eastern banks. They would fight the Sioux and Cheyenne tribes. The number of Indians in the tribes had been miscalculated to General Custer, and every last soldier was killed.

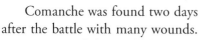

Comanche was found two days after the battle with many wounds. He was so weak he could barely stand. Pocked with arrows and bullets, he was in bad shape. The saddle had turned under his belly. The blanket and pad were missing. One of the rescuing troopers was about to cut the horses' throat, but a Swede soldier named Gustave Korn dissuaded him.

Another soldier saw Comanche in a clump of trees and was ordered to shoot him. He did not have the heart to carry out this order when the horse whinnied. Gustave Korn asked to care for the horse. He and some other men took Comanche to the river. They bathed him, dressed his wounds, and led him 10 or 12 miles to the Far West boat where Captain Marsh fixed up a stall between the rudders. By the time the boat reached Fort Lincoln, the horse could not walk, so they carried him to the stables in a wagon and there supported him with a sling. He mended rapidly.

Comanche was treated as a hero. He was given the freedom of the fort's grounds. He was saddled for all engagements and official occasions, but he was never to be ridden again. Comanche became a national celebrity. On ceremonial occasions, Comanche walked at the head of Keogh's old troop, draped in black mourning.

# The Two Soldiers Of Fortune,
# The Horse And Soldier

*This is an exciting true story that began in the 1800's. It introduces you to the famous war-horse that didn't have a name at first. Later on this war-horse earned a name because of his participation with the Comanche Indian and Custer's Battle. Myles Keogh was a swashbuckling soldier of fortune who bought this horse to replace his horse that was shot in battle. After reading this story you will read the continuing stories in the History section which tells the story of the horse's life of being a war-horse with the Seventh United States Cavalry*

Myles Keogh was a swashbuckling soldier of fortune. He was a tall handsome Irishman with dark fringed smiling blue eyes, which made many a lassie's heart flutter. This mercenary was a native of Ireland, a son of an officer in the Fifth Royal Irish Lancers. Myles attended Dublin University, but a restless adventurous spirit caused him to quit after two years. He decided to follow in his father's footsteps and joined The French Army. At the time the French Army was fighting against the fierce Arab tribesmen in North Africa. Several friends and he took off for Algeria. That is when he first became acquainted with the African Barbs who were said to be cousins of the fabulous Arabian steeds. To him they were ugly and small and churlish animals. He was used to sleek Irish hunters and big cavalry mounts of his father's regiment. After mounting the Barbs, he learned that they were one of the toughest and most courageous breeds he had ever ridden. These spacious deserts with palm fringed oases, and veiled beauties were all that a young man could dream of, but then a call came to him from another part of the world.

Italy was having trouble and the Pope sent an appeal for Catholic youths to come to their aid. Four of his comrades and he joined the Papal forces. They were commissioned in the Battalion of St. Patrick in the summer of 1860. Although this small army, poorly equipped, fought bravely, they were against hopeless odds. The Pope himself awarded Myles Keogh the medal, "Pro Petri Sede."

After this venture the war between the northern and southern states was going on. Keogh and his friends sailed for the United States and joined the Army. After serving in major battles and receiving the brevet rank of Major he was transferred to the Western Theater commanding the mounted forces of Sherman's army. In July 1866, he was a commissioned captain in the newly organized Seventh United States Cavalry, with brevets of Major for Gettysburg and of Lieutenant Colonel for the war. Keogh served for two hard and demanding years. His dandyism appearance made him very unpopular with the hard-bitten Western troopers. Captain Theodore Allen of the 7th Ohio Calvary said, "We did not like the style of Captain Myles Keogh. There was altogether too much style. He was a handsome young man as I ever saw. His uniform was spotless and fitted him like the skin on a sausage." The other officers and soldiers soon changed their opinion when Keogh led the Buckeyes in a charge during the Atlanta campaign. Battalion and yelled, "Hip, hip hurrah boys! Here we go!"

After joining the 7th Cavalry, Keogh covered miles and miles of the forever plains of Western Nebraska, Kansas and eastern Colorado. He had a brush with some Kiowa Indians, and his horse Mike was shot from beneath him. He then had a horse called Paddy, but never used him in battle. Paddy lacked the endurance that Keogh had expected from his size and build. He needed a war-horse, a horse with some mustang blood in him. The talk of the regiment was "That wild Irishman can't hold onto his money, but he sure knows horseflesh." It was known that he could outride anyone in the regiment, anyone but General Custer.

April 3rd, 1868 the government bought forty-one horses, and was unloading them from the train at Ellis Station. Keogh looked on at the bewildered and frightened horses. Some of them stood with drooping heads.

Others were milling around in a state of confusion and finally finding the water trough they drank thirstily. A young trooper approached him, saluting and said, "Captain Sir! What horse are you interested in?"

Keogh measured the horses with his eyes and then he pointed to the buckskin. In his Irish brogue, he said, "I've had my eye on that Bucko over yonder. Don't you think so?"

"Sir," the young man said. "I'd pick that handsome chestnut over yonder for an officer's mount. That horse you're looking at has a rough coat sir." That was true the horse's coat was rough, and there were burrs throughout his mane and tail.

Keogh laughed, "Horses are like women, you don't always go by the outside appearance. He's a little small but take my word for it, he's the best of the lot. Look at the way he holds his head, his broad chest, the length and the line of his back." His voice trailed off and adjusting his hat to a cocky tilt he slipped under the fence of the corral. With a spring in his step he walked towards the claybrook sorrel gelding, part mustang, with a black mane and tail. He weighed about 925 pounds and 15 hands. There was a devil-may-care glint in this particular horse's eye's that had caught Keogh's attention. Keogh reached up and stroked the horse's dust filled mane, whistling a lilting Irish tune. He rubbed the animal's neck and along his withers and back. The horse was taking nervous short breaths. "You're my kind of horse, Bucko," Keogh said. Then his firm hand slid down the stretched neck then traced the white star on his forehead down to his velvety nose. With his other hand, he reached into his pocket and drew out something holding it in his palm at the horse's nose. Sniffing the aroma of apple bits, the buckskin gently took them with his lips nibbling on them. Keogh said in a low voice, "Ah you like these chunks of apples." Keogh turned and looking at the sergeant, who was staring at him disbelief, said, "This is the horse I want." He gave the horse a pat on the rump. The horse and master had met at last. There was no hint of a historical happening eight years later for these two soldiers of fortune, which would be a day of infinity.

It wasn't long until the first saddling of the horses began. Keogh's horse was use to gentle handling and he accepted the burden of the saddle, after giving it a good shaking with good humor. Keogh adjusted the saddle to the horse, not the horse to the saddle. Keogh didn't mount his horse to begin with but leaned heavily on him to get him use to the pressure. Finally one beautiful day Keogh said, "Today's the day, my Boyo." Talking all the while he took the reins and put his footed boot in the stirrup very smoothly, then he swung his other leg over. He was in the saddle. Boyo stood frozen as in shock, then he became a bucking bronco! He bucked. He leaped into the air. He jumped sideways to remove this added weight. Then he set off across the spacious plains at a wild and furious gallop. Keogh sat firm and gave Boyo full rein. "That's my Boyo, run like the wind. Show everyone what you're made of!" They became one, the spirited Irishman and Bucko. After a good run, he turned him until he ran in a great circle back across the drill field. When the horse slowed down, Captain Keogh drew him to a stop and dismounted. He rubbed Boyo's neck. Then he gave him some apple bits. Without warning again he swung himself into the saddle. The horse tossed his head and danced a little, while the captain guided him once more around the drill ground. This time the horse performed as Keogh expected him to. He had learned to gallop true to lead off with the right forefoot when bearing right, with the left when bearing left. Then sailing over the corral fence, Keogh gave him full rein across the vast prairie. Keogh's teeth flashed under his jet mustache. When they came back to the coral, he dismounted and commanded Comanche to lie down.

The horse became proud to be part of the best troop in the finest regiment in the West, Troop 1 of the Seventh United States Cavalry. This good-natured horse soon became a favorite of the men. While the men played poker in their spare time, Bucko would drink a couple of beers and nudge some of the men on their backs.

In the fall of 1868 Keogh rode his well-trained horse in the battle with the Comanche Indians on the Cimarron River on the Beaver Fork. The horse was struck in the hip by an arrow. He reared up neighing, but the Captain did not realize the horse was injured and continued to fight from his back until the battle was over. Afterward, he discovered an arrow broken off in the horse's rump. The wound was treated, and after the horse recovered, he had earned the name of Commanche for his guts and bravery in continuing to carry his master despite his own pain. He was never again called "Bucko."

In a story written by Margaret Leighton, which is reasonable factual, a trooper called McBane said he saw the arrow strike. "He sure squalled as loud as any Comanche. I never heard a horse let out that kind of a hollar. A sure enough Comanche yell."

Keogh replied, "Comanche! That's the name for my horse."

Again in 1870 during a battle against the Comanche Indians, Comanche was struck in his leg. He limped for over a month, but soon recovered. In 1871, Comanche was wounded in battle once more, this time in his shoulder. Again, he recovered quickly. Comanche was the talk of the Calvary. This tough, fearless, soldierly horse continued to go into battle despite being wounded many times. Most other horses would have become battle shy with incidents such as this, but Comanche seemed to look forward to a battle with his master, Keogh.

On June 15, 1876, the Seventh Cavalry and Indian scouts were mounted ready to participate in the biggest battle of their lives. The band on its gray horses pranced and played, 'Gary Owen', the unit's battle song." Custer and his 7th cavalry marched into Fort Lincoln and across the parade ground. It was an impressive sight, although the morning was foggy and cold. The Arikara scouts were in their outlandish finery beating their war drums. Next marched the Seventh led by their officers in a column of platoons. The colorful flags and guidons snapped in the wind. Spurs and bits glistened and jingled. There was a brief halt while married men said goodbye to their wives and children. There was a chill in the air as the men and mounts disappeared in a white cloud like mist. Some of the women and Indians felt this was a premonition. The gallant men were headed into another battle, the last battle of the Bighorn. They would fight the Sioux and Cheyenne tribes. There was an unforeseen problem. The amount of Indians in the tribes had been miscalculated to General Custer. The Indians killed every last soldier in Custer's unit. Comanche was found two days after the battle with many wounds, near his master. Most bodies had been decapitated, but Keogh's was not. It was thought that the cross on the chain with the wording Agnes Dei, which meant the Lamb of God, worn around his neck had protected him in death. The Indians thought it was medicine.

Comanche was pocked with many arrows and bullets. The saddle had turned under his belly, and the blanket and pad were missing. One of the troopers was about to cut the horses' throat but a Swedish soldier named Gustave Korn dissuaded him. He said he would care for him. They took Comanche to the river and bathed and dressed his wounds. Then they led him about 12 miles to the Far West boat where Captain Marsh fixed a stall between the rudders of the boat. When they arrived at Ft. Lincoln, the horse was unable to walk. The men carried him to the stables in a wagon and there supported him with a sling. The tough war-horse mended fast. In the spring of 1878 Comanche would move about without help. The cavalrymen said, "Comanche is the second commanding officer of the regiment." From that day on Comanche was treated as a hero. He was given the freedom of the fort grounds. At all engagements and official occasions, he was saddled. He could never be ridden again. Comanche became a worldwide celebrity and the pet of the regiment. With all of his old fire and gutsy spirit, he took his place at the head of the troop and went through the drill formations faultlessly. On ceremonial occasions, Comanche walked at the head of Keogh's old troop draped in a black mourning net. He had a pair of Calvary boots slung across the saddle with the toes pointing backward.

Then another catastrophe happened that changed Comanche's life again. His health had been good, and his keeper, Gustave Korn and he had a wonderful relationship until Gustave was killed in the battle at Wounded Knee. No matter what the new attendant did after that, Comanche became increasingly depressed and ill. He no longer rooted through garbage pails. The beer weakened him. In fact he turned his nose up at it and did nothing except lie gloomily in the barn or in a mud wallow. On November 7, 1891, his ears twitched forward and his limbs trembled...With a low wicker, Comanche joined his captain.

But this isn't the end of Comanche's story. The officers of the 7th Cavalry wanted to preserve Comanche. They decided to give Comanche to the Dyche Museum, and property rights are now vested in the University of Kansas through the generosity of Lewis Lindsay Dyche. This living legend now stands, well cared for at the University of Kansas in a humidified glass case receiving thousands of visitors from all over the world annually.

*Author Notation: This next story is for Young at Heart readers. Some of the nonfiction part of this story really happened with a love story of two young people, one a young girl of seventeen, and one an Airforce soldier. It involves the Pearl Harbor War story, some of it nonfiction and some of it is fiction. Go back in time with me to the 1940's and enjoy this clean, romantic, humorous, story. It was fun being in love with this man who put up with me. We were married for 50 years. He died at our 50 th Wedding Anniversary Party at our church. I know he is in Heaven, and I plan on sneaking in heavens back door as the love of my life waits for me.*

# A Military Love Story

Dedicated to the Love of My Life...Wil Shumway

Standing on a hill in the midst of oak trees in a rural community called Avon was a two-story white brick farmhouse with a wrap-around porch and a much used swing. Green ferns hung gracefully from the porch eaves. On the East Side of this house was a rose garden with hybrid roses. This home had been in the Koehler family for generations.

A young girl of seventeen by the name of Akisha, her mother Ella, and her father, Shad Koehler lived in this small peaceful community of about 3,000 people. Nothing ever happened in this city to disrupt the peace, just the regular events of weddings, new babies, and social events which kept the telephone lines busy. Akisha was an early riser. She crawled out of bed and tiptoed down the stairs to the porch to her thinking place, 'The Swing'. The

48

swing gave her moral support many times when problems arose. And right now she had a dilly of a problem. As the swing rocked back and forth gently, she closed her blue eyes feeling the light breeze blow through her long hair. Taking deep breaths she inhaled the sweet fragrance of the rose scented breeze. Stretching her long legs out, she let the swing slowly coast to a stop. Crossing her arms, she hugged herself tightly as she trembled a little thinking about living on the brink of disaster and disobeying her father. Getting up from the swing she stepped out on the dew covered soft grass. She closed her eyes and twirled around and around until she fell dizzily on the soft green carpet of grass. She giggled softly. Something she had dreamed about had happened last night, but not in a way she had expected. Lying on her back, she gazed at the deep azure never ending sky, mixed with wispy, cirrus clouds. Oh she had never felt this way before, not in all of her 17 years. Was it because she had disregarded Papa's strict rule? How was she going to tell mama and papa what happened? Or would she keep this secret locked in her heart forever? She knew that her heart was the most hugger-mugger place in her whole body. And best of all she was the only one who held the key. Yes she would freeze the memory of last night until she was alone, alone as she was right now. She would keep the adventure of last night locked in her heart forever!

Her mother's voice broke the silence as she called out, "What in the world are you doing lying on the grass with that good dress on? You'll get grass stain on it."

In a teasing voice, Akisha laughed, "Oh Mother, my dress is green, and it won't show anyway."

Shaking her head with a slight smile of amusement, her mother continued. "Don't forget to clean your room before you meet Marsha." Ella was carrying a cup of coffee in her hand as she always did in the mornings and sat down in the swing looking at her precious daughter. She thought how hard it had been for Shad and her to conceive a baby. When Akisha was born, there wouldn't be another baby for them. Maybe they had spoiled her and were a little protective, maybe too much so, but she was the light of their marriage.

Akisha sat up. The sun cast its light through the trees. With her long fingers she combed through a cluster of clover with their purple blooms beside her. She gasped. Right in the middle of the clover was a four-leaf clover. This was an omen of good luck. Picking it she opened the locket she had around her neck and slipped it inside. Springing to her feet and brushing the grass from her dress she said, "Oh Mother, reality! It's not any fun."

Papa who had overheard their conversation stood in the doorway. He said, "Well reality, my dear has its good moments. It puts meat and potatoes on the table."

Looking at him with a slight pout on her face, she sighed, "Oh, Papa, adults just don't understand teenagers. Were you and mama ever worry-free?"

Walking over to the swing, Papa sat down next to Ella and put his arm around her. He whispered in her ear softly, "I sort of remember a day like that. Don't you dear?" Ella snuggled up to him and smiled.

Akisha looked at them. They were such a loving couple. Would it be a good time to tell them what happened last night? No, it might spoil her day. She would do it at a more opportune time. As the day went on, Akisha hurriedly cleaned her room. She had promised Marcia she would meet her at the bus station and see the romantic movie with Clark Gable in it. After she cleaned her room, she sat down at her vanity, looking into the mirror. Putting her elbows on the glass top and resting her chin on her hands, she decided she would put her shell pink lipstick on. She quickly puffed some powder on those frightful freckles, which sprinkled across her nose that Papa called sun kisses. The Grandfather clock in the hallway struck 12 chimes. The bus would be pulling up at the corner in 5 minutes. Snatching her purse from the bedpost, she ran out the door, calling "Goodbye" to her parents. Out of breath after running down the hill, she reached the country road just in time. The bus was pulling to a stop. Fumbling in her purse for her ticket, she stepped onto the bus giving it to Big Eddie, the bus driver. The bus was a military bus, and as usual was crowded with soldiers. She paused searching the young masculine faces for that certain one with the vivid blue eyes. Fort Harrison was an army base a few miles down the road. Whenever she went anywhere, she had to ride the only transportation available for the suburban communities. The young soldiers always looked forward to her appearance. Sometimes they burst out in the popular song, "Oh you great big beautiful doll."

Pursing her lips she quickly sat down, so no one would see the dimpled smile that was ready to exit from her full lips. She always sat in the seat behind the bus driver, Big Eddie. Not because she wanted to, but it was orders from headquarters from her father that she always sit there. Her family attended the same church as he did. Shad Koehler and he had served in the navy together. Eddie knew why Shad was so protective of his daughter, but he didn't like to think about it. Shad would say to him, "We had a very private, peaceful community, until the Air Force Base moved in Ed."

Big Ed always answered saying; "Well there's a thorn in every rose Shad. But it brings extra dollars to our community."

Being the town banker, Shad could not deny that. He always replied, "Humph." Akisha was not to talk to those soldiers. She had been brought up to be a dutiful and an obedient daughter whenever her father gave her definite commands. She could hear her father's stern voice now. "They're from all over the world, even Timbuktu. It's peacetime now. They need to stay home with their families."

Akisha never questioned her father. She knew that he had served in the Navy protecting his country, and he had a slight limp to prove it. There were medals in frames hanging on his study walls, but noone talked about how he got them.

As she sat on the bus, she blocked off the steady flow of talk, and in a dream state, her mind wandered to last night when Marsha and she had gone skating. She could hear the music blaring now, as they walked into Skateland. They skated round and round the rink holding hands. With a jaunty air of freedom, they skated faster and faster with the air whipping through their streaming hair. But then the moment was scarred. Their church minister, Dr. Shellenberger was there. To her he was an older man, as old as her Papa almost. He reminded her of Ikabod Crane in the story of 'The Legend of Sleepy Hollow'. He always wore the same black suit, like he was going to preach or attend a funeral. She was so embarrassed when he whizzed over to her and took her hand in his. He never asked her if she wanted to skate with him. His prim wife didn't skate. She just sat on the sidelines with a frozen smile on her lips. Akisha knew she was miserable just sitting there while her husband skated off in the midst of the kids. If she saw him in time, she would skate off and pretend she didn't see him. She liked seeing him on Sunday mornings in the pulpit preaching. That's where he belonged, she thought to herself. When she discussed this problem with her mother, Ella would only smile and say "Akisha, I hope you treat him nice. He and his wife were born in these parts and we all grew up together. They weren't lucky to have children like the rest of us did, so we share our children with them. He is human too."

When her mother talked to her like this, she often thought, Why didn't I take after my sweet lovable mother? Instead she wanted to say that skating was just for kids, not for ministers, but she kept her thoughts to herself. It just wasn't fun being a girl sometimes! That is until last night. Reality was so confusing. And sure enough, after Marsha and she stopped to rest, up skidded Reverend Shellenburger coming to an abrupt stop, stirring up a little poof of dust from the rink floor. Just to humor him, she extended her hand before he attacked it. He smiled his toothy grin and pulled her out on the rink. The song was a bebopper, 'In The Mood'. They began doing a two step around and around the rink, with a little fancy kick there and a little kick here, (not bad for a minister, she thought). As they twirled around the edge of the rink, she noticed a handsome soldier standing on the other side of the guardrail watching them. He was looking straight at her, not at the minister, but at her. Would this song ever end? It would die down, as if it would end, and she would start to skate off the rink floor, then it would begin all over again. Those eyes, from beneath that soldier's cap, were the bluest she had ever seen. They were fringed with dark lashes. She wished he would ask her to skate. Not that she would., but father wouldn't know. But maybe… As they circled the rink, she couldn't help but glance at him and noticed he didn't have any skates on. His hat was pushed back showing his tousled blond hair. Her heart raced and began doing flip-flops. She couldn't breathe. She had never felt this way before. Was the old saying, "Love at first sight true? Was this reality?"

The Reverend had to steady her. "Are you ill Akisha?" She placed her hand on her forehead. He led her off the rink, sitting her down by his wife, Malinda.

"Darling," Malinda said, "you look peaked. Tommy, Go get a wet towel."

Marcia skated over to them, with her dark eyes even wider than they usually were, with a look of concern on her face. Placing her arm around Akisha's shoulders, she said, "You look a little ill. Maybe a chocolate Coke will make you feel better."

She really didn't want anything to drink or eat, but Marcia always thought a chocolate Coke would cure everything, especially if Don Sloo made it.

Rev. Tommy brought a wet towel handing it to his wife.

Sister Malinda wiped Akisha's face with it. Sitting down by his wife he put his arm around her. Marcia and Akisha just stared at them.

That was the most human thing they had ever seen the Reverend do. Maybe mama was right, Akisha thought, and before she knew it, she blurted out. "You are human after all, aren't you?" They all laughed. Thanking the minister and his wife for their concern, they headed towards Rossiter's Drug Store. When they walked through the door, Don Sloo was at the soda fountain. When he saw the girls come in, he immediately began making two chocolate Cokes. They hopped on the high stools at the mahogany, marble-topped soda fountain bar resting their feet on the polished brass foot rail. Marcia watched him as if she were in a trance. The whole town knew Marcia had a crush on Don. As they sipped their Cokes, Akisha nudged Marcia in the ribs telling her to hurry or she would miss the bus. Marcia lived in town and didn't have to ride the Military bus. The bus was waiting when they got to the station. Akisha remembered that Big Eddie wouldn't be driving the bus tonight. He had the weekend off. She felt daring. She knew the rules her father had set down about the soldiers and the bus. For the first time in her whole life, she decided to sit in the middle of the bus. There were several soldiers on the bus already, except for one elderly woman. She sat by her. Getting on the bus and walking right by her, was the same blue-eyed soldier who had been at the rink. When she saw him, their eyes met. He smiled. She lowered her eyes, afraid that he would think her brusque. Her face became flushed and hot. She became lightheaded. She would be glad to get off of the bus into the fresh air, where the breathing would be easier. The back of her seat moved. Oh no! He sat in the seat directly behind her. She folded her hands in her lap, trying to be composed. She wanted to look over her shoulder at him. She was much aware of his physical presence. Excitement electrified her insides. It seemed an eternity before she saw the white picket fence in the moonlight. If they ever removed that fence, she would never find her way home. That meant that her street was at the next corner. "Excuse me," she said to the woman as she stretched over pulling the cord. The monotone sound of the bell silenced the low mummer of voices. She was usually afraid of the dark because the tree branches silhouetted in the light of the moon made them look like witch's long fingers, but tonight she wasn't thinking about witches. She walked at a slow pace enjoying the thoughts of her evening. She knew she would never see him again, and if she did, they would not be able to get acquainted. The porch light of her house shown likes a beacon. The door was unlocked.

A voice from the bedroom called, "Is that you Akisha?"

"Yes Mama, I'm home." It didn't take her long to go to sleep. She and Marcia were going to the movies tomorrow afternoon. The next morning she hurried to catch the bus. Akisha would be waiting for her for another ordinary day at the movies. Walking through the bus station, she grabbed Marcia's hand, saying, "There he is talking to that man in uniform."

Bugging her eyes out Marcia said, "Who? Oh no! It IS him! Just calm yourself down Akisha. Pretend you don't see him." They quickened their pace, with their high-heeled baby doll shoes clicking noisily on the marble tiled floor.

"Well hello there!" a deep masculine voice rang out, echoing throughout the station as they walked by him.

Without thinking, Akisha said, "Hello Big Boy."

Marcia looked at Akisha in shock, as they walked faster towards the door, and down the sidewalk towards the movie. They heard steps slapping the pavement getting closer and closer. Someone tapped her on the shoulder. It was the soldier. He was breathless. Akisha hesitated.

In an authoritative voice Marcia whispered, "Keep walking. Don't pay any attention to him."

"Excuse me." He was keeping pace with them. "You're the girls who were at the skating rink last evening."

Looking at him, Akisha's mind went blank. She was thinking, Oh he's so tall and those broad shoulders. Marcia nudged her. Quickly she said, "We don't talk to strangers. Please go about your business, or we will call that policeman over there." She raised her hand and pointed her manicured finger at a policeman who was directing traffic with his billy club.

Ignoring her threat, he said to Akisha, "I have been looking for you ever since you got off of the bus last night."

What audacity, she thought. The nerve of some people, doesn't he know that she meant business? Not monkey business.

Akisha stopped walking and placed her hands on her hips. "Why would you be looking for me Soldier Boy?"

He chuckled, "Well I saw you skating, and I said, "Self, that's the woman I've been looking for all of my life." He looked at her in amusement. "We rode the bus together. Don't you remember? When you got off the bus, I vowed to myself that I would not rest until I found you again!"

Akisha drew a deep breath. She retorted hotly. "What made you think I would want to see you again?"

Ignoring her question, he continued. "When you got off the bus, I couldn't quit thinking about you. In fact I dreamed about you all night. This morning the General and I drove all around the countryside looking for you."

"Oh?" Her eyes narrowed and she looked at him in a suspicious way. "You and your General go around looking for girls?" She laughed a low musical laugh. "What a line that is, but I have to give you credit. It is a different approach. I can see why my father won't let me have anything to do with the Military."

He looked miffed. "I happen to be a chauffeur for the General, and he wanted to come to town, so as we were coming down 38th street, we turned where I thought you got off the bus last night. I guess you think that's funny too!" A scowl covered his handsome face. "And what's so bad about soldiers anyway?"

Marcia, who had been standing idly, tapping her toe on the pavement and rolling her eyes up towards the sky grabbed Akisha's hand and said, "We're going to be late to the movie."

Just then the policeman walked over to them. "Is this guy bothering you girls?"

Before Akisha could respond, Marcia, her brown eyes, looking wider than ever behind her thick glasses quickly replied, "Yes he is Sir!"

Akisha looked at the soldier. The chemistry was there. There was a magnetic charm about him that attracted her to him. Marsha elbowed her.

She tried not to look at Marcia, who was staring at her as if to say, "Give him the killing answer."

Akisha stuttered. "No, no, he isn't officer. He…he just thought he knew me."

The officer laughed. "Well if I was young and single, I would think I knew you too." Swinging his Billy club, he winked at the young soldier and walked away whistling.

The young soldier stared at her in disbelief. That's what I was looking for in her, he thought. She's not only good to look at, but she is her own woman, a spunky one at that! "My name is Glenn. Do you mind if I go with you, wherever you're going?" He stared at her with those eyes.

Glancing at Marcia, she took a deep breath. She tried to say convincingly, "Well Marcia, since we're not complete strangers, I don't see that it would hurt for him to go with us."

Marcia's mouth flew wide open and her usually wide eyes, narrowed. She looked at the soldier with hostility.

"Only under one condition though," Akisha continued.

"Oh?" With his eyebrows arched, he asked, "Conditions?"

In a firm voice, she said, "We all go Dutch. No strings attached. Then after you go to the movie with us, we will go our separate ways, and never see each other again."

"That's a pretty tough condition, Why would you want to do that? Our paths are bound to cross again since you ride the military bus."

"Well I hate to begin our friendship like this, but my father has never let me have anything to do with anyone in the military."

Glenn said, "I won't ask you why again, but in that case I guess, I will have to agree, so I can go with you, even though it is only for a day."

Akisha's green eyes saddened and in a distraught voice she said, "I don't know why either. It has been one of the mysteries in my life, but my father always has a good reason for everything." Stretching her hand out for a handshake, she said, "It's a deal then?"

He took her hand, but remained silent. When she went to pull her hand away, he held it for a few seconds more than he should have. She thought to herself, I hope I made the right decision.

When they reached the movie, he paid for the tickets. "Since this will be the beginning and ending of a beautiful friendship, I would feel like a heel if I didn't take you both to the movie." In an elegant sweeping bow he said, "This way my new friends." He led them through the theatre door.

Marcia bugged her eyes. Looking at Akisha she leaned over and whispered in her ear, "You've just put another peg in your coffin, Akisha."

Akisha knew this was true, but she wasn't going to spoil these priceless moments. This would be a chapter in her life that she would never forget! Her life would go back to normal tomorrow, but now she just wouldn't think about it. Later she would have lots to write in her diary.

Everything went well at the movie, although she did feel a little uneasy in the love scene parts with this young man sitting beside her. She felt his arm across the back of her seat.

By the end of the movie, even Marcia felt comfortable with him, so comfortable, that when Akisha and she went to the restroom to freshen up a bit, she grinned slyly, and said, "Wouldn't it be funny Akisha, if he started liking me instead of you?"

Akisha looked at her and said, "What about Don Sloo? You would sure miss those chocolate Cokes." They both doubled up in laughter.

After the movie, they stopped at Rossiter's Drug Store. As usual, on a Saturday evening, the place was jiving with their school friends. The jukebox was playing. There was only one ice-cream table and with three chairs left vacant. Glenn pulled out the chairs for them, removed his Air Force hat and sat down. Scanning the menu, he said, "A chicken salad club sandwich sounds good to me, how about you?"

Marcia's friend, Don Sloo came to wait on them. She spoke up saying, "You know what we want Don. Akisha and I want two chocolate Cokes. You're the only one who makes them the way we like."

Don's face and ears grew red and he quickly made an exit behind the soda bar. While they were waiting for their food, Marcia tried to make conversation by asking, "Tell us about your family Glenn."

He replied in an abrupt way, "I have no family."

Chills ran up and down Akisha's' spine. Marcia was at a loss for words, which was unusual for her. There was an uncomfortable silence. Don Sloo came balancing the tray and acting stupid at the right moment. As he served them, teetering with the tray of food held high in the air, they began to laugh. He said, "Are you going to church in the morning Marcia?"

In an agitated voice, she said, "Don't I always go to church Don?"

Ignoring her, he said, "Who's your new friend?"

"Oh," Akisha said. "This is Glenn. We met him skating."

He stretched his hand out, pumping Glenn's hand up and down. "Hi Glenn, Glad to meetcha. Have these ladies bring you to church tomorrow."

"Oh, do all of you go to the same church?" Glenn asked.

"Yes," Marcia said, "we've gone to the same church since we were in Cradleroll together."

Looking at the big clock on the wall, Glenn said, "We had better go. The last bus for the night is about to leave." He paid the bill.

This time they didn't embarrass him and offer to pay. Taking the money from Glenn, Don's ears colored up again. Taking a big gulp he said, "Marcia I'm getting off work now. Since you don't live far from me, why don't I drop you off at your house."

Marcia's eyes bugged, and she choked on her gum. "Is it all right with you Akisha?"

Glenn answered saying, "Go ahead Marcia, don't worry about Akisha, she's in good hands."

When they arrived at the bus terminal, their bus was pulling out. Akisha laughed as Glenn ran and flagged the driver down to stop. Thank heavens Big Ed wasn't working tonight.

Glenn led her to the very back seat. He reached over and took her hand like it was a piece of Dresden china and held it. He said, "I don't suppose we will ever see each other again."

She didn't reply. She bowed her head and a tear trickled down her cheek.

Taking out his handkerchief, and gently lifting her face he wiped the tear from her face, saying "Never? Never is a long time."

Wonderful sensations began sweeping through her body. They both were silent for they knew this was the last time they would be together. Tonight she hated seeing the picket fence in the distance. Reluctantly she loosened her hand from his and turning her head towards him she said, "There's the picket fence Glenn. My stop is the next one."

The bus lights were still dim. An instinct of exceeding strength urged him to kiss the vague sweet mouth. For him and his kind of a kiss on a girl's lips was no slight thing. Pulling her to him, Glenn bent his head and their lips met. She started to pull away. After all, you just don't kiss a man you hardly know on a sort of first date, she thought. But the passion of a first kiss and young love took over. The kiss seemed to go on forever. Slowly releasing her he reached up and pulled the buzzer. When he turned to look at her, she had already walked up to the front of the bus. She never did like good-byes.

Getting off the bus, she put her trembling hands on her hot cheeks walking as fast as she could up the drive to her house. She didn't look back. When she reached the front door she quietly walked in, tiptoeing up the stairs to her bedroom. She didn't undress. She flung herself on the bed sobbing uncontrollably into her soft pillow. She felt years older than her youthful age of 17. She had disobeyed her father for the first time in her life. She had finally grown up, and she was miserable.

When she left the bus, Glenn moved with his army buddies to the vacant long seat in the back of the bus. One soldier said. "That's quite a gal Glenn. Why didn't you get off of the bus with her and take her to her door?"

"Well for one thing, I would be stranded." Trying to act indifferent, Glenn said, "And boys there is a problem. Her father has something against the military. We can't see each other again."

Red, a boy from Tennessee, with a full face of freckles and a smile that stretched clear across his face, said with a southern drawl, "Well Glenn, looks like y'all sort of liked each other. What did that guy say? Let me think. "Ah think he said, "Darn the torpedoes, full speed ahead!" Everyone cracked up.

Glenn looked at him, and in a matter-of-fact voice said, "I aim to marry that gal, Tennessee, and nothing is going to keep me from seeing her again!"

"Yahoo! That's the ole spirit buddy, I'll dance at your wedding!"

Akisha woke up to a feeling of apprehension. Stretching her arms, she climbed out of bed. She still had her dress on. Out loud she said, "Thank heaven it's another day, a new day to get control of my emotions and tell my mother and father what I did." Gliding into the bathroom in a statelike dream she stepped into the shower, lifting her head up letting the warm water cleanse her body and mind. She felt much better now. What did Grandma Dorn used to say? "Time heals everything." Just then, her mother called, "breakfast is ready."

She could smell the chocolate gravy now, her favorite breakfast, but only on Sundays. After all she had to watch her figure! Throwing her bathrobe on, she held on to the banister, partially sliding down.

Her father sat at the kitchen table reading the Sunday paper, and slowly drinking his coffee. Looking up at her over his hornrimmed glasses, he said, "Well good morning, my Princess."

She walked around the kitchen table and lightly kissed him on his cheek. Her mother came to the table with a large platter of biscuits and chocolate gravy. They bowed their heads in prayer.

It has to be now, Akisha thought. In a tone of urgency, she cried, "Papa! Mama! I have something to talk to you about. Something that's very important to me."

"Now eat your breakfast, dear," Mama said calmly. "This conversation can surely wait until after church."

His mustache twitching, and looking at his watch, Papa said, "Jumpin Jerusalem, we had better hurry, or we will be late."

She knew not to continue her conversation, especially when Papa's mustache twitched. Papa would be very angry if they got to church after the doors were closed, and the services were started. Akisha gulped her food down, wiped her mouth with the linen napkin, saying, "Excuse me." Running up the steps to her room, she decided to wear her pink silk dress with her sassy pink heels to match. The horn honked. Her mother would be upset. She did not like for Shad to blow the horn.

When they pulled up to the church, Marcia stood chatting with Don Sloo. Shad let his family out while he parked the car. Marcia and Akisha went to the choir room putting their robes on and talking with their friends. Soon it was time to follow the choir director to the choir section. Standing up they quickly opened their songbooks. Bobbing her head back and forth to the rhythm, Sister Blythe's fingers danced up and down the keyboard playing 'That Old Rugged Cross.' Looking out at the people one could see women wiping tears from their eyes. Akisha and Marcia always thought this was unusual.

At the end of the song, Dr. Shellenberger, with a spring in his step went to the pulpit saying, "Sister Blythe, you put a lot of spirit in that good old song." Someone yelled, "Amen!" Pastor Shellenburger began his sermon. As always Akisha's mother and father sat with the reverend's wife, Sister Malinda, Marcia's family and Big Ed with his wife. Everything was in order, as it should be Akisha thought. Then the door leading into the sanctuary creaked open. Marcia whispered, "Someone needs to fix that door."

Akisha, who had forgotten to remove her chewing gum, swallowed it choking. Her heart was beating like a drum. The blood drained from her face. Clutching Marcia's leg, she began praying in a whisper…"Dear God help me survive what is actually happening right now."

Coming down the isle was Glenn, searching for a seat.

Dr. Shellenburger paused staring at him. There was only one seat left in the whole church. Glenn sat down beside Mr. Koehler. Mr. Koehler's mustache twitched.

Later Akisha said she didn't believe anyone remembered a thing about the Sunday service after Glenn walked in. It was the longest service she had ever endured. Marcia agreed.

At the end of the service, the choir shuffled back to the choir room. Marcia said in a worried voice, "Our secret sat next to your father, Akisha."

Shaking her head sadly, Akisha said, "I tried to tell my parents about our meeting with Glenn, but they didn't have time to listen this morning. I never dreamed he would come to our church."

"Well I hate to say I told you so." Marcia said. "Don Sloo and his big mouth about attending church." She patted Akisha on her arm.

Just then Sister Malinda stuck her head in the choir room door calling, "Akisha and Marcia, the reverend wants you both to come to his office. He has a surprise for you."

Marcia taking Akisha's hand, said, "Let's march to the guillotine. It looks like a day full of surprises, and I'm as much to blame as you are." She grimaced as if she were in pain. Akisha moved her hand in a slashing motion across her throat. Marcia was such a good friend. When they walked in, Akisha's mother, father, and Glenn were talking with Pastor Shellenberger.

Looking up with an elated Godly smile on his face, the minister said to Akisha, "Look who's here, the soldier from the skating rink. This is a small world isn't it?"

Akisha stared at Glenn. She thought he looked rather sheepish, or maybe it was a guilt complex look. She walked over beside her mother. She needed her mother's protection! Her father was glaring at her. "Hello Glenn," she blurted out. "Oops!" She covered her mouth.

Shad had a scowl on his face. He looked hard and fierce. His mustache twitched nervously. "How in tarnation do you know his name, daughter?" Her father was losing control. Big Ed walked over to his side putting his hand on Shad's shoulder. "Steady Shad."

Akisha began stammering and saying in a hushed voice, "That is what I wanted to talk to you about this morning at the breakfast table, Papa. "Oh Papa, I have broken your trust, and I am so sorry. Please forgive me." Tears streamed down her face.

Shad held his trembling hands to his side.

In a clear brisk voice, Glenn said, "I knew your family went to this church Sir. Akisha and Marcia didn't know I was coming."

Then he took a deep breath with beads of sweat popping out on his forehead. "Sir, I am to blame for all of this. I am here, because I wanted to date your daughter. I wanted to get your permission first." Looking at them with unsmiling eyes, he continued. "Don't blame her, sir, it's not her fault. She told me from the first minute I saw her that we could never be friends or see each other."

Shad said. "What's your name boy?"

"Glenn, sir! And Sir, do not refer to me as a boy. I am nineteen years old."

Shad's muscles in his neck flinched; his jaw was set. But then his eyes softened as he looked into this young man's eyes, looked at him as if remembering something. His mind went blank. It was another time.

Big Ed walked over to his side, putting his arm around him. "Shad, you okay?"

Shad, shook his head, as if to clear it. Ella took Akisha by one arm and Marcia took the other arm gently and walked her towards the door. Ella said, "I think we need to leave dear." As they went through the door, Akisha took a lacy handkerchief from her purse, dabbing her tear filled eyes. "Oh mother, this is the worse day of my life. I hate him. I'll never speak to him again." She began sobbing. Her mother held her close. As they left the church, Akisha dried her tears, and looking up at her mother, she said, "He did try to protect me Mama by taking the blame. Oh Men!"

Meanwhile, Pastor Shellenburger motioned the men to sit down. Shad spoke first, "Ed, look at this young fellow. Look at those eyes. Those heavy fringed lashes. Who does he remind you of?"

Big Ed gave him a knowing stare. Shad looked down at his hands, which were folded in his lap. In a choked up voice, he said, "You and I both know Ed who this boy is. The ghost of the past has come back, come back to haunt us, to let us never forget what happened that morning at Pearl Harbor.

Shad jumped up from his seat pounding his fist against his other opened hand. In a somber voice, he said, "It was December 7, 1941 in the Pacific. The air raid alarms were screaming. Fiery fragments were pouring down from the sky as bombs burst. Pearl Harbor was turned into a Bay of terrible explosions, smoking ships, flames and death. Men's heads, like sitting ducks were bobbing in the rolling ocean amuck with thick crude oil. Thick smoke fogged the air. We were surprised and outnumbered by the Japanese."

Glenn sat there woodenly as if he was in a state of shock. Then he jumped to his feet. "What are you two talking about? What about Pearl Harbor?"

With an intent stare, Shad said, "Son, who was your father?"

In an irritated voice, Glenn said, "What difference does that make Sir?"

Shad grabbed him by his shoulders, shaking him. "Just answer me. I need some answers son. NOW! It's important!"

Glenn's voice trembled in anger. "My full name is Glenn Ethan Lance, Jr. My father Glenn Ethan Lance, Sr., was an officer in the United States Navy stationed in Pearl Harbor. He was killed aboard the battleship Arizona sir, December 7, 1941. Arizona is his watery grave. That's all I know Sir!"

Shad's face paled and a sudden twitch of the muscles in his tense face showed that he was under extreme stress. He grabbed Glenn close to him hugging him with tears streaming down his face. "Son, Son, he cried, "Big Ed and I knew your father. We served with him in the South Pacific. I was with him on the Arizona the day he was killed!"

Glenn clasped his arms around Shad laying his head on his shoulder. They stood there for an endless period sobbing.

Dr. Shellenberger fell to his knees praying incessantly. In praying, he said, "This is the providence of the Lord."

In a hoarse emotional voice, Shad continued. "I need to tell you something Son. Something I have had to live with everyday of my life, since that dreadful day!"

Just then a knock came at the parish door. It was Sister Malinda. She wanted Shad to know that the Smith's took Akisha and Ella home to prepare the Sunday dinner.

Shad spoke up and said, "Malinda call Ella and tell her to set another plate at the table. I am bringing our son home with me."

Then he turned back to Glenn. "Tell us how you happened to join the Air Force Son."

Glenn sat back down in his chair, hunched over with his cap in his hand. He ran his fingers through his blond hair. "You knew my father? I can't believe it. I was very young when he was killed. There weren't any pictures. My grandmother would never talk about it. All she said was my father and mother died while in the Navy while serving at Pearl Harbor. After she died I joined the service. My intentions were to go to Pearl Harbor to retrace my father's and mother's steps. I read every article about Pearl Harbor I could lay my hands on. Then I read about the Japanese man who dropped the bomb on the ships." He jumped out of his seat. Raising his fist in the air, he angrily cried, "I won't be satisfied until I meet with him and tell him all the pain I've endured, not having a father growing up, never having a dad and mother at my football games or my graduation. And most of all not having a mother to comfort me. All because of that damn war with the attach by the Japanese."

All the men sat back in their chairs listening, shaking their heads over the young man's bitterness. Shad was shaken to see this clean-cut young man fuming with pent up emotions over a war which was long past. And then, he knew he had been wrong these many years with his pent up feelings too wanting to keep Akisha safe from ever associating with anyone in the military.

Shad got up slowly unknotting his tie and walked over to Glenn's side. He began talking in a hushed tone. "No, Son, I know how you feel, but that was war. Each man had his reasons for fighting. Ed and I knew your father and mother. I received the Purple Heart, the Medal of Bravery that should have been your fathers."

Big Ed butted in. "No Shad, I won't let you take the blame. You deserved and earned that medal given! You were blown well clear of the ship that day. Though you were partly paralyzed, you swam, detouring to help shipmates along the way."

Shad said, expressionless, "Let me talk, Ed. I have to get this out into the open. The night before that fateful morning your mother and father, Glenn, Katrina, Big Ed, my wife and myself went to the navy ball. We were young. We danced and partied the night away.

"Yes!" Ed chimed in. "Katrina and Glenn won the jitterbug contest that night. Your mother, son, even took her shoes off afterwards. Her feet were killing her. Boy those two could really dance! Yes that was a night to remember! After the dance that night, we drove down to the ocean beach and sat on the moonlit shore watching and listening to the sound of the waves beating against the shore. Your mother and father were so in love, Glenn. They often talked how they were going to send for you to join them. They called you their little 'tuff nut'."

Shad said, "Do you remember Ed, the oyster shell that was lying in the sand next to Glenn? He picked it up opening its shell, and there lay a beautiful pearl."

"How could I forget anything about that glorious night Shad. Yes I remember. In the moonlight, Glenn turned to her and pressed the oyster shell with the pearl in her hand. I can still see the emotion in her face and the moonlight shining on her beautiful blond hair as she looked up at him. She was so beautiful and both of them were so in love."

"Your father son, with an adoring look at your mother said, "This pearl stands for our eternal love. We will never be parted in life or in death. "Tomorrow sweetheart we will go to the jewelers and have it set into a ring."

"Shaking his head, Shad said, "Little did any of us at that time realize the impact of that statement. It would haunt us forever."

Everything in the room was still. Turning to Shad, Glenn said, "You said sir, that you were to blame. What did you mean by that?"

Shad began talking, "After the pleasant Oceanside evening, the women dropped us off at Battleship Row. We were on duty that night on the Arizona. It didn't take us long to go to sleep. Good food and a relaxing evening with our loved ones, and the gentle rocking of our ship lulled us into a deep sleep. Early in the morning, a tremendous explosion brought us to our feet. The radio blasted out "Air raid on Pearl Harbor. This is no drill." As the messages were sent out, Japanese planes were diving on the main target, Battleship Row. Then a bomb hit our ship. In minutes oil was gushing from our ruptured ship, parts of it bursting into flame. A wall of fire surrounded us. Just after the explosion, we heard the commander's voice, "Abandon ship." Pausing and wiping sweat from his brow, he continued. "Everyone stampeded towards the compartment ladder. Glenn and I met at the foot of the ladder leading up through the turret to safety. I was behind Lantz, but he said to me mockingly, "After you, buddy." We laughed even then in our dangerous situation. I shook my head no, but he pushed me ahead. Not looking back, I didn't realize it, but he shoved several of the other men ahead of him too. All along I thought Glenn was behind me. When I ascended to the utmost round of the ladder, I looked behind me and found that Glenn and the other men were not there anymore. Turning to go back looking for him, another huge explosion rocked our ship. I remember being blown off the ship and seeing a huge spray of stars. When I came to, I was covered with black slick oil and was being whipped around in a turbulence sea battleground. The vengeful waves slapped and snapped as they swooshed forcibly against my body." Shad was reliving the moment. Beads of sweat popped out on his face. Hesitating and drawing long sharp breaths, Shad continued. "Desperately I bobbed around looking for Lantz, calling to him. Then there was a tremendous explosion, and I saw the grand old Arizona sinking to its watery grave. I knew that it took the crew with her including your father!" Then pausing, silence prevailed as Glenn's body shook convulsively as he sobbed. Shad put his arms around him until he became quiet.

In a rasping voice, Glenn choked out, "I'm sorry, I just can't help myself. These emotions have been pent up for so long. I know a man shouldn't cry."

Shad said, "Son you are one of the finest men I have ever met. You are definitely your father's son. His spirit is in this room. This didn't just happen. It was God's plan. Now I have a son we've always wanted."

Pastor Shellenburger was still kneeling in prayer. He stood up and in almost a whisper he said "Shad how in the world did you survive?"

Shad said, "I don't remember anything after the last explosion. When I came to I was in the hospital."

All the men in the room embraced each other. Glenn looked at all of the men and said, "A big load is off my shoulders. After hearing this, I realize that my thoughts about getting even with the man that dropped the bomb on my father's ship was not good thinking."

"Big Ed patted him on the back and said, "It's good that a man can admit he is wrong."

Shad walked over to Glenn and said, "I have been wrong too Glenn. This has been a great learning lesson for me also. Because of me my daughter was fearful of having anything to do with the Military."

Pastor Shellenberger raised his hands in the air, saying, "Praise the Lord! It's been a day of miracles!"

Shad rose from his chair. "Come on son, the women will be waiting with dinner. There's more to this story. Ella, my wife was a nurse and worked with your mother, Katrina at the Base Hospital that was bombed."

Meanwhile when Ella got home from church, she quickly put on fried chicken, then mysteriously escaped to the attic. When she came down the stairs, she had armfuls of books. When Shad and Glenn drove up, Akisha, Marcia, and Don were playing croquet on the spacious lawn. Akisha ran over to meet them. All of them went into the house together. The girls set the table while the men sat in the parlor talking. Ella put the dinner of fried chicken, mashed potatoes, macaroni and cheese and creamed peas with homemade yeast rolls on the dining room table. For dessert, Marsha and Akisha made sundaes with Don assisting. Glenn could not take his eyes off of Akisha. He said, "So this is what family is all about."

Ella spoke up and said, "We are your family now Glenn. We now have a son."

Shad spoke up saying, "Akisha you now have a brother."

Glenn said, "Excuse me sir? I will never be Akisha's brother."

After dinner, the men retired to the parlor again. Ella had placed scrapbooks on the coffee table. She sat down, and looking at Glenn she said, "I want you to look at some of pictures of your Mother and Dad, Glenn. We were great friends. I had the night off from working at the base hospital, but your mother was scheduled to work the night shift. Early the following morning, the hospital was bombed, and there were no survivors. Shad and I have not looked at these pictures since the Pearl Harbor incident.

Akisha walked into the room with a large bowl of popcorn and sat next to Glenn as her mother talked about the pictures. After looking at the pictures, Ella said, "We always wanted a son, and we have finally found us one Shad." Walking over to the stone fireplace, Ella took a velvet blue case from the mantle and handed it to Glenn.

Glenn said, "What's this?"

Ella said, "It's something your mother and father would want you to have. That night after your father found the pearl in the oyster and handed it to your mother, we left the men at the ship. I dropped her off at the hospital. Before she went in, she said to me, "Ella, take this pearl home for me, so I don't lose it. In the morning Glenn and I are taking it to the jeweler's, so it can be made into a ring for me." She had it wrapped in this lace handkerchief. It has been there ever since. She would want you to have it Glenn."

Very carefully Glenn opened the handkerchief. There lay an oyster shell with a beautiful shining pearl in it. His eyes glistened as a tear rolled down his cheek. Without saying anything, he tucked it into his pocket.

Shad walked into his office and came back with a glass-framed picture. It was the Purple Heart he had been awarded for his bravery. He said in a hoarse voice, "Son this belongs to you!"

Glenn held it for a long time looking at it without saying anything. Finally he looked at Shad and said, "Sir, I cannot take this. You earned it, and my father would want it this way." They hugged one another.

In the deepening dusk Don and Marcia left. Akisha and Glenn walked to the porch watching them drive down the winding driveway in Don's old jalopy. They sat down in the swing. He reached over and took Akisha's hand into his. They both sat there for a long time listening to the evening sounds of the frogs and soulful cry of a mocking bird. They heard the screen door open. Shad walked out on the porch. "It's getting late Son. I'll drive you back to the base tonight." He went back into the house to get his keys.

Glenn looked at Akisha. He said, "Can you believe how things changed so completely in just a few hours?"

She looked at him in the moonlight nodding her head. He took her into his arms and kissed her.

After Shad and Glenn left, Akisha watched them drive down the moonlit driveway. Akisha knew there was more to come of their relationship. In a dreamlike state of bliss she went into the house and slowly climbed up the stairs to her room and began writing in her diary.

# The Members of the Greely Expedition in 1881

Members of Lady Franklin Bay Expedition, 1881

We listen to the weather news on the radio or television about what the weather will be almost every day. We never think of how the weathermen get their information. How do they know if it's going to rain or snow or be a wonderful day? How or what events made this possible to get this information?

Well it all began more than a century ago, when twenty-five young, handpicked soldiers and two Eskimos accompanied Lt. Adolplhus Greely on a scientific mission to the Arctic, which began so high-heartedly in 1881 and ended with such stark tragedy.

These men collected valuable meteorological, tidal, and magnetic data, carrying out faithfully their share of work outlined by the international Circumpolar Congress. For over 100 years the data collected by various members of the Congress have been the source book for students interested in magnetism and meteorology.

Today navigators, telephone, telegraph and cable engineers, and geophysical prospectors rely on magnetic instruments to locate oil, nickel and other minerals lying beneath the earth's surface. Those natural forces directly affect radio and aeronautical engineers.

One of the heroic men was my Great Uncle Julius Frederick. He was born in Germany in 1851. His parents brought him to America when he was 2 years old. The family settled and grew up on a farm four miles southwest of St. Mary's, Ohio. His childhood was shortened when his mother passed away with the flu and his father remarried.

When only seventeen years old this young teenager with a restless spirit ran away to Chicago, Illinois with only one dollar in his pocket. The self-reliance that stood him in such stead in his later adventures was then formed.

In 1876 Frederick enlisted in the regular army at Cleveland, Ohio. He was first stationed at Jefferson Barracks at St. Louis, Missouri and was then transferred to Ft. Ellis, Missouri, where he was assigned to Troop L of the Second Cavalry. Because of his courage on the Western Frontier with the Sioux and Nez Perse Indians, he was chosen for the Greely Expedition. For 5 years he fought in various Indian campaigns under Colonel Nelson A. Miles, a self-made soldier who dressed in a bearskin coat and wore a beard protecting his face from the cold. This period of Frederick's life is replete with bloodcurdling experiences with the red men of the Western Plains. He was poised under the dreaded-scalping knife, and many times he escaped miraculously. Several times he encountered hand to hand battles with the unprincipled warriors, only to escape with a whole body and clean record for bravery and valiant service. Private Frederick soon became known as a chunky short man in stature and a tough quiet soldier whose actions spoke louder than words. An officer asked him one time, how he came through the battles with the Indians unscathed.

In his slow talking manner, he replied, "I don't know whether I killed anybody or not, but I guess I did for I was scared and fought hard, and the way it was you couldn't keep from killing somebody if you didn't get killed, and I'm still alive."

He was involved in the Muddy Creek Battle, but before that his Troop L Battalion of the Second Calvary was called to assist General Custer in fighting the Indians and their Chief, Sitting Bull. General Custer decided not to take Sgt. Frederick's platoon, as he thought that he had enough men. His decision backfired and Custer and his men were massacred by Sitting Bull and Crazy Horse's band. Luck had followed Frederick again, but he and his soldier buddies would not rest until they tracked the red men down and fought the last battle at Muddy Creek revenging the ones that had slaughtered the well liked and respected Custer and his few men. Frederick was noted for his bravery in The Lame Deer Fight of May 7, 1877 (also known as the Muddy Creek Fight). He never forgot that battle and seeing a terror stricken buddy who tried to surrender to an Indian by handing his carbine to a warrior. The warrior beat him senseless with it. All Frederick would say was, "That Indian is now in his happy hunting ground."

After that came the momentous period of his life. Arrangements were being made for the Lady Franklin Bay expedition to the polar region. The expedition's purpose was to report weather observations, such as the wind, tide, temperature, pressure magnetism and gravity in the unexplored virgin land, the Arctic, which is now Alaska. This played a crucial role in determining the weather of the temperature zone. It was commonly known as the Greely expedition, as it was under command of Lieutenant A. W. Greely of the Fifth Cavalry. It was a government enterprise and the government was anxious that no men except those physically perfect should be members of the expedition. A careful search was made of the men who were in the service. Rigid physical examinations were held. Private Frederick had volunteered for the expedition, impelled by his love of adventure and was accepted as a physically perfect man with an excellent record of bravery. The tragedy began as a grand adventure.

The team consisted of 25 U.S. Army men led by Signal Corps Lieutenant Adolphus Greely and two Eskimo hunters. Eskimos Jens Edward and Frederick Thorley Christianonsen were chosen because of their knowledge of the Arctic.

In 1881 the explorers were sailing on the Proteus boat. This was a sealer of 467 tons as part of an 11-nation International Polar Year study of Arctic weather from St. Johns Newfoundland.

The American explorers manned the northern most polar camp; a mere 500 miles from the then unexplored mysterious North Pole. They called their camp Lady Franklin Bay. They were prepared to remain in the Arctic for two years. Plans were made that a ship would be sent in 1882 with food, and if it was prevented from reaching them because of heavy ice it was to land on a depot as near them as possible. Another ship, the Proteus, was to pick them up in 1883 for the return voyage.

At Lady Franklin Bay there seemed to be plenty of game, elder ducks, musk oxen, seal, bears, and walruses. It was thought the expedition would experience little trouble in remaining there for an indefinite length of time. Frederick had unusual talents, as did the other men. This could have come from being born to German parents who were from Germany. He made pens from barrels to protect 4 young calves. He also made the men sleeping bags from blankets and canvas.

For enjoyment Roderick Schneider entertained the men playing his violin. His favorite song to play was 'Over the Garden Wall.' They also had shooting matches, foot races, and wheelbarrow races and played baseball. One of the explorers, Charles Henry won the shooting match November 30, 1882.

Besides these sports, they enjoyed going exploring and hunting, which was a hunter's paradise. There were plenty of musk oxen, and the fishing was unbelievable. Jens, the Eskimo and Explorer Connel caught a large salmon weighing 4 ¾ pounds at Lake Alefondra. Explorers Cross, Ellis and Brainard went on a five day hunting trip to Cape Beechey. They killed 8 musk oxen and 22 geese. They had to strip to their skins and swim the icy cold streams. Eskimo Jens also shot an ermine near Musk Q Bay. He also shot a musk ox that weighed 363 pounds. It must be said, that all the men learned from each other's skills, which helped them, cope with the far North. The two Eskimos, Jens and Fred taught the men many things, including some of them their language. Also the men learned quite a bit about the Eskimo dogs. An Eskimo seems to enjoy nothing better than making an unruly dog or two acknowledge him as master. Roderick Schneider enjoyed this immensely because he loved dogs. The men were all like brothers to one another.

One day Long and Jens went down to open water. Long was standing on a piece of ice floe and it broke from the main body of ice and drifted out to sea. Jens saw Long's dilemma and paddled out to him in his kayak. Long urged him in vain to return to fast ice and save himself. The loyal fellow refused to obey and explained in his simple way, "You go, me go too."

They read and estimated temperatures when mercury was frozen solid, when spirit thermometers were sluggish and inaccurate. Frederick took astronomical observations while the midnight sun was still 10 degrees below the horizon, correcting for refraction against cloudbanks at various temperatures and computer humidity at 60 degrees below zero when his mustache was stiff as a statue. The explorers learned weather observation under extreme stress. The men were overwhelmed when a glorious aurora covered the whole horizon with blinding lights. The richness and vividness of colors and tints, then sudden bursts of violate forms took their breaths away. The curtains were accompanied by spectacular streamers, which ran to the highest altitude of the heavens changing into various forms. This was an introduction of a magnetic story. The aurora held the men spellbound for more than twenty minutes in temperature of 66 below freezing point. It was an experience of grandeur that the men never forgot. The expedition spent 3 years far above the Arctic Circle, farther north than any white man had ever lived so long before. Sergeant Frederick was in the party that succeeded in reaching a point farther north than any other expedition had accomplished. In April 1882, a party of ten men, commanded by James B. Lockwood left Fort Conger where the entire expedition had passed the winter with instructions to explore the northeastern coast of Greenland. Julius Frederick was one of the men whose assignment was to drag the sledges for the party as the dogs that had been taken with the expedition had been sadly depleted by disease. Therefore the men were forced to do their work. At intervals along the way, stations were established where food was left for the return trip and at one of these stations, the last established before the northern end of the trip. Private Frederick was placed in charge. It was for this reason only that he was not with the party that at last forced its way to the northend of Lockwood Island, 83 degrees, 23 minutes and 89 seconds. Many hardships were experienced during the trip, but at last the adventurers returned to the camp of the main party. They gathered valuable scientific information and explored wide areas. But they were left to face a terrible ordeal when the ship that was to take them home, the Proteus, got trapped and was crushed by ice and sank in July of 1883. Its crew reached Greenland in open boats.

When the ship failed to show up as planned, Greely the commander of the expedition, carried out prearranged emergency plans moving his men to an alternate pickup 260 miles south to wait for relief at Cape Sabine. This southern camp was on Pim Island near Ellesmere, overlooking icy Smith Sound. The retreat from Conger to Cape Sabine involved over three hundred miles travel by boats and one hundred with sledge and boat; the greater part of which was made under circumstances of danger. Arriving at the southern camp with less than 40 days of food, the men learned for the first time of the sinking of the Proteous nearby. At this time the men were alive and healthy, but according to pre-arrangements, if Greely and his men were not picked up in 1883 they were to go southward where there was supposed to be food caches. When they arrived to that destination, there was hardly any cache of food.

It was at Camp Subine that Frederick showed most plainly the stuff of which he was made. He was an excellent hunter. There was a polar bear sitting on an iceberg eating a young seal. When he saw Frederick he got on his feet, a monster of a bear weighing about 600 pounds roaring loudly, echoing throughout the Ice Mountains. Frederick aimed his rifle and brought him down. When he got back to camp, he was a hero.

When their food ran out the men had lived on boiled sealskins, strips from their seal skin clothes and shrimp. Frederick was the man. On account of his well-known fairness, the task of distributing among the men the meager rations were allotted to him and Private Francis Long. To avoid all disputes as to any claims of favoritism these two men took the plates of food that had been considered the scantiest by other members of the expedition and in numerous ways showed their unselfishness at a time when selfishness is most likely to develop.

As food became scarcer, the suffering from starvation became greater. Frederick petitioned to be allowed to go in search of more beef that had been cached sometime previously a number of miles from Cape Sabine. He believed that he could find the meat. It was plain to all the members of the party that if it could be found the lives of the members of the party could be saved. An effort was made to dissuade him from the attempt, but "No" was not in his dictionary. It was pointed out to him that the effort could only end in his death, but he insisted specifying that he should receive the same rations for the journey as were being served to the men in the camp. At last Greely gave him his consent. Greely said, "This was the stamp of this man."

Julius and Sgt. George W. Rice started with a sledge for the place where they thought the meat was cached. Sgt. Rice, weakened by the scant rations for so long, was unable to bear the strain of the journey. Private Frederick stripped his own coat from his own shoulders and wrapped it around the feet of Sgt. Rice with little protection of his own body. Sergeant Rice died in his arms. Frederick then scraped a shallow grave in the ice and buried him.

Several days later Frederick staggered into camp. With him he brought the rations that were Rice's unconsumed share. Despite the hard journey back to the camp and the weakened condition on account of lack of sufficient food, Frederick ate only the rations that had been allotted to him so his comrades might have the remainder.

The crewmen of the sunken ship had survived, and one of them left a note at the southern cape before the sailors fled home in a small auxiliary vessel. "Everything within the power of men will be done to save you."

Meanwhile when word of the sinking of the rescue ship reached Washington, Army and Navy bureaucrats lashed over who was blamed for the ship's loss for 20 days about how the men were to be rescued. The brave American explorers were left to die horribly of starvation and exposure in the frigid Arctic while Washington bureaucrats squabbled over their fate. In December, President Chester Arthur ordered an Army-Navy board to draw up rescue plans. The President went to Congress to get funds for the rescue. Finally the crew of the Bear ship, commanded by Lt. Wm. H. Emory, U.S.N. actually effected the rescue. The ship Thetis commanded by Commander George W. Coffin, J.S.N. brought up the rear in event the Bear or Thetis or both was unsuccessful.

Finally in December, President Chester Arthur ordered a joint Army-Navy board to draw up rescue plans. A month later, the plans were ready, and President Arthur went to congress to get funds for the rescue. A bickering congress hummed and hawed for 25 more days with one lawmaker even demanding that instead of buying rescue ships, they should be built from scratch in his home state.

The Bear had a long and successful career while a commissioned ship in the United States Coast Guard and United States Navy in 1884. It was built in Scotland in 1874, and purchased for this expedition by the United States Navy in 1884. In the 8 weeks it took to reach the men, 10 more explorers died of starvation and exposure. Meanwhile, the seven men left had given up hope of ever being rescued.

These last few men survived the horrors of Arctic winters, with scant food, shelter, and clothing. They were without fire, light, and warmth. They faced intense cold and bitter frost, slow starvation, insanity, and death.

Through all of this torture even the men who had died kept a complete record of their findings. Along side of each man was a small bag containing his last will and testament, a sentimental message and a momento of the North to the one he loved best. Carefully stacked in the middle under a heavy stone were all of their scientific data. This included maps, geographical data, photographs, notes on fauna, and flora weather statistics, and charts of more then 1,400 miles of the coastline of Northern Greenland. Also there were first maps of Ellesmere Island and accounts of first views of the Western Ocean, now the Arctic. Also there was a discovery of a mountain range and vein of coal, fossils of one time and tropical vegetation within 10 and latitude of the North Pole. There were also artifacts of early man and statistics of certainty that the white man cannot survive the Arctic without supplies. Explorer Henry Biederbick was sent to the interior of Grinnell Land to explore for a practical route to the westworld. He returned with the discovery of a large lake extending across Black Rock Vale. As far as he traveled, he took frequent magnetic bearings and meteorological observations. These records had been carefully conveyed from Lady Franklin Bay to Cape Subine, more than 300 miles, by sheer strength. They kept and preserved them while they drifted helpless for 34 days on an ice floe in the Kane Sea.

Near midnight, June 22, 1884, Sgt. Frederick and his comrades heard a faint whistle of the rescue ship USS Thetis. When the rescuers reached the men, they were dazed and emaciated, found in blown down frozen tents. Some of the victims had to be chopped from their sleeping bags. Along the side of each man was a little bag containing his last will and testament, a sentimental message and a memento of the North to the one he loved. Frederick's belongings had a tattered Bible in it. He had never lost his faith in God.

Sgt. Julius Frederick was the only man rescued who could stand. Weighing only 108 pounds he pulled himself up by his frozen bootstraps and mustered a staggering salute. He insisted upon walking abroad the rescue ship, the Thetis. Only 6 of the 7 survivors made it home. The seventh man, both hands and feet frozen off, died at sea tragically missing the hero's welcome given for others.

The rescue was of great hardship. No ship had ever penetrated as far north as early as June that had been able to accomplish this feat. Members of the rescue party were volunteers from enlisted men and commissioned officers of the U.S. Navy. They were selected for their knowledge of the Arctic. During the last few days of their journey, the crews faced severe storms, wind, snow, ice and freezing rain in order to complete their mission. They performed their rescue mission with great credit and honor.

August 1, 1884 was a beautiful summer's day in Portsmouth, New Hampshire, when the ships arrived about noon. Thousands lined the shores of the Pisvataqua River waving flags and banners and shouting, "Welcome Home!" The City of Portsmouth arranged a reception and parade with a possession of 2,000 men and seven bands.

When Julius Frederick returned home he married his sweetheart and had two daughters. He settled down in Indianapolis, Indiana where his family was. My Grandmother, Mrs. Koehler and his nieces and nephews lived down the street from his family.

He obtained a position with the United States Weather Bureau and worked there for seventeen years.

But this is not the end of this story. For many years after the ill-fated Arctic trip, Julius still had a strong desire to return to the North Pole by a dirigible balloon. His name came up once more prominently before the public April 9, 1903.

Mr. P. E. McDonald of Chicago, Illinois conceived the idea of reaching the North Pole by means of an airship or a dirigible balloon. This idea found that Frederick gave him staunch support. Frederick was positive that North of the 80th degree there was plenty of game and considerable vegetation. He argued that the animals and the birds in the Arctic migrated to the North instead of the South when the winter approached. From his experience he was convinced that of all known manners of travel that the airship was the only feasible way to reach the Pole. He willingly agreed to accompany Mr. McDonald on his trip. He specified that the efficiency of the airship should be thoroughly tested.

In August of 1903 Mr. McDonald came to Indianapolis, Indiana and discussed the plans for their journey. He was anxious to beat Commander Peary.

Sgt. Frederick's dream to go back to the land he loved so much was not meant to be. He died of cancer in January of 1904.

Julius Frederick and his friends of the Greely Expedition paved the path for future explorers. Not only did they set up a meteorological research station in the virgin Arctic; they discovered several new regions, including parts of Ellesmire Island. The explorers of the Greely Expedition pilgrimed the paths of a virgin land to a new frontier for America, Alaska!

## BOOK ACKNOWLEDGEMENTS OF PEOPLE THAT HAVE ALWAYS BEEN THERE FOR ME FOR MY ESCAPADES

The First Woman Mayor of Greers Ferry, Arkansas, Shelly Davis

Jan Stratton, Illustrator and Hair Stylist

Wanda Biggs, Proofreading Specialist

Brian Carpenter, Computer Specialist

Carl and Jean Garner

Financiers, Arthur and Richard Shumway

Sandy, Susan, Florence, Betty Shumway, refreshment caters

David Lee, Publisher, The Sun Times

Lori Thompson, The Sun Times

Louis Short, The Sun Times

The Arkansas Democrat Gazette

The Fairfield Bay Crew Newspaper

Greers Ferry Police Department

Greers Ferry Fire Department Crew

Greers Ferry Ambulance Crew

Higden Post Office

R&R Sanitation's crew

WHBQ Radio Station

Lee Bell, A security officer for Salt Cave Drive Neighborhood

Jerry Davis, Historian, known for his fabulous
collection of historical pictures.